PICTURE BOOK PERIL

ST. MARIN'S COZY MYSTERY
BOOK 10

ACF BOOKENS

1

The wind was so cold that I thought I might be blown away, but fortunately, I had three dogs weighing me down. My hound mix Mayhem, my basset hound Taco, and Sasquatch, my friend's Scottish terrier, were sniffing along like it wasn't twenty-five degrees outside. In fact, Sasquatch looked like he had just come into his element—which, genetically, I guess he had.

I knew this ruse of durability would pass as soon as we returned home, though, when all three canines would suddenly become frail, shivering messes who needed to sleep the day away by the fireplace.

And to be honest, I couldn't blame them. This December was colder than the previous ones I'd experienced in St. Marin's, and I was resenting it hard. My rule was that if it was going to be this cold and gray, it had to snow. Unfortunately, the climate hadn't bowed to my dictatorship as of yet.

So after a few blocks of endless sniffing and urinary greetings to the rest of the neighborhood dogs, I tugged the pups toward home. Once inside, they ate, drank a bit of water, and, as

predicted, took to their beds by the fire as if they had just survived a trek to the North Pole.

I, however, had to get to work, so I filled my to-go mug with coffee, shouted a "see you later" to my still-sleeping best friend down the hall, and returned to the bitter wind for the walk to my bookstore.

All Booked Up was coming into its third holiday season, and I was determined it would be the best ever. Given how disastrously a store-based Santa had gone the year before, I worked with the other shop owners to set up our new Santa in an empty storefront up the block. Now he had his own space, a staff of volunteer elves from the local Ladies Auxiliary of the VFW, and responsibility for the children who came through.

I glanced into his shop as I walked by and smiled. Even without Santa and his elves, the space sparkled with magic. Twinkle lights flickered off glitter-infused snow, and Santa's chair was made from wood and painted like candy canes. It was gorgeous.

Just a few doors up, my front windows were coming along quite nicely, too. For some reason, my assistant manager, Marcus, decided our theme this year would be a steampunk Christmas, so he was constructing an elaborate clock interior in one window. Here we would display various Christmas titles, including Dickens's *A Christmas Carol* and a fun newer book, *Hauntings and Humbug*.

The other window was going to be a steam train inspired by *The Polar Express*. It would be a childhood winter theme that included some Christmas books and titles for Hanukkah, Kwanzaa, and the general winter season. My shop had a reputation for being ultimately inclusive when it came to its offerings, and I wasn't going to let my own love of Christmas exclude anyone.

A little bell tinkled as I opened the door of the former gas station that I had converted into a bookstore. I looked over to

see Rocky, the owner and manager of our in-house coffee shop, already behind her counter, stocking what appeared to be peppermint scones. If I knew Rocky, and I thought I did, she would have set one of those aside for me for when I go over in a bit to get my morning vanilla latte. I couldn't wait.

First, I needed to do my opening chores, including walking through the store to ensure everything was in order. I closed up the night before, so I didn't expect any surprises. But of course, I had learned over the years that in St. Marin's, surprises were something I needed to learn to expect.

Fortunately, this early December morning brought nothing out of the ordinary. The shelves were in good order, and the throw blankets I'd commissioned from my friend Henri, a weaver and artist, were still casually hanging on the backs of most of the chairs. We hadn't done a lot of holiday décor inside the store this year, but I decided to do my best to make this space as warm and inviting as possible.

We'd even gone so far as to install an electric fireplace in the new addition to the store. I found two secondhand leather club chairs at a local consignment shop, and now, that corner was a favorite reading spot for most anyone who entered the store. I loved that because while I appreciated every purchase a customer made, I wanted my store to be a place where people knew reading of the merchandise was encouraged.

I ran my hands over the teal and purple throw that Henri had woven before turning on the fireplace and heading back to the counter to log onto the register and see what email had reached us for the day. The owners of the shops on Main Street were planning a major holiday bazaar for next weekend. I knew the other shop owners would have been exchanging plans and ideas all night while I was enacting my new "no phone after nine p.m." rule.

I was right, too. A lot had happened in the last twelve hours, and it was all exciting. Apparently, someone found a business with a team of actual reindeer who would come and allow children—and adults like me—to pet and feed the reindeer. And Elle, our local farmer, offered to do a wreath-making class in her shop, sending every participant home with an evergreen wreath. This bazaar was shaping up into a big deal, and I was glad because, in a waterside town, sometimes even the winter holidays didn't spur enough foot traffic to help us all turn a profit.

I was eager to hear more about Rocky's plans to have a cookie decorating competition sponsored by her café, so I headed that way. I tried to act nonchalant and ask her how her night had been, but she called my bluff.

"You saw the scones, didn't you?"

Lately, Rocky styled her hair in long crocheted braids that trailed down her back. Last weekend, she had them redone with strands of red and white that made her look all the more festive, especially when she applied her favorite crystal rhinestones at the corners of her eyes. With her light-brown skin, beautiful cheekbones, and all the festivity, she could have been one of Santa's elves. Although, her Olympic-level snark might not have been appreciated by the Auxiliary ladies.

"I'm that transparent, aren't I?" I said as I ran my fingers through my now bright-red curls. Rocky inspired me to go bold for the holidays. "People from miles around look at me and go, 'Harvey Beckett. She's the one who loves a good pastry.'"

"There are worse things to be known for," Rocky said as she slid the porcelain plate with the glazed goodness to me with my super-huge mug of caffeine.

"Thank you," I said as I tapped the top of her register to remind her to add this to my charge account. Most months, the accounts we ran with each other's businesses pretty much canceled each other out since I loved coffee just about as much as Rocky loved books, but I didn't want her trying to slip me free stuff. She was taking online classes toward her MBA, and I knew they weren't cheap. "No free gifts, even for friends." It was a rule Rocky and I had both taken on in the past few months as we attempted to grow our businesses.

I carried my scone and latte back to the register, savored a bite and a sip, and then went to turn on the neon open sign in the window. Ten in the morning and time to go, even though I didn't think we'd have our first customers until closer to lunchtime, when Rocky's amazing sandwiches, a new addition to her menu, drew in some of the local lunch crowd. Still, consistency was the key to any business.

With the store open, and a scone waiting for me, I settled behind the register to eat and read for a few minutes. This was one of the perks of owning a bookshop—reading on the job was required. My latest book, *We Should All Be Millionaires* by Rachel Rodgers, was one Rocky had recommended. It was a great book on building a business and wealth that incorporated one of the most important things: social justice. Rodgers made the case that women with wealth gave it back and empowered other people, particularly other women, to get ahead. I loved it so far.

A few minutes later, my scone gone and my latte just dregs, I decided to begin the weekly task of picking titles for returns. I always felt a little sad pulling these books off the shelves and sending them back to their publishers. I wanted to save and treasure every book, but that wasn't feasible economically. Even with the addition to the store, I didn't have room for every book I'd like to carry, so a few had to go back each week.

I was making my way through the craft section and pondering how the recent surge in cross-stitch books was interesting when I heard the bell over the door jingle. I stepped out so I could be seen by whoever was shopping and smiled when I saw the face of our newest Main Street shop owner, Carson Radison.

Carson, or Car as he told everyone to call him, had moved

to St. Marin's over the summer to open a clock shop. It was such an old-fashioned store idea that I knew it would be an instant success in St. Marin's, and given that Car was a skilled horologist, he had quickly built a reputation on the Eastern Shore as the man who could repair any clock or watch.

Car was built a bit like a leprechaun, an image I swore he courted with his wool sweater vests and bow ties. His graying red hair and beard added to the overall effect, and one day, I wouldn't be surprised if his voice took on an Irish lilt.

"Good morning," I said as I walked over to give my neighbor a hug. "How are you? Staying warm?" It was a cliché to talk about the weather, but it was a universal topic for a reason—it bound us all together.

"Oh, I love brisk days like this. Feels like home." I had no idea where Car's home was, but given his appearance, maybe he was actually from the North Pole. "I came to ask a favor, Harvey."

"Sure thing. Let's sit. Want some coffee?" I asked him as I pointed to two wingback chairs in the fiction section that gave us a place to talk while letting me keep an eye on the store.

"I'll get some in a bit. Thanks." Car wrung his hands together in his lap. "This may be a bit out of line, but I thought it wouldn't hurt to ask."

I rolled my eyes because I literally could not think of anything Car would ask that was out of line. He was such a gentle soul. "Please. I'll do what I can."

"Okay," he said nervously. "Would you consider adding my collection of Victorian-era clocks to your steampunk display?" He looked at me and continued, "Marcus told me yesterday that you were doing one, and all night, I couldn't shake the idea that my clocks would be a good fit."

I smiled and nodded vigorously. "Are you kidding? I'd love that, and I know Marcus would, too. What a great idea." I was already imagining how we'd elevate some clocks and pair others with books. "Bring them over anytime, and we'll add them in. We'll make a sign, too, that talks about the collection if you want to write something up."

Car tapped his feet excitedly against the floor. "Wonderful. Thank you, Harvey. I'll bring them over later today if that's all right."

"More than all right, Car," I said as I followed him toward the café. "Marcus or I will help you carry them over if you'd like."

"That would be great. What time does he come in?" Car asked.

"Noon," I said. "One of us will be over just after."

"Perfect," he said and smiled at me before turning to Rocky and ordering a black coffee and a scone. She was going to be out of those by the end of the morning.

Surprisingly, the next couple of hours were busy. Our favorite customer Galen came in with his bulldog Mack, and they spent a couple of hundred dollars, their usual, on cozy mystery books.

"Have you heard about Finlay Donovan?" Galen asked me as he set both books of that series on the counter.

"Heard of her? Please don't tell me I know something more about a mystery novel than you do, Galen?" I said as I bent down to give Mack a good scratch under one of his many chin folds.

Galen laughed. "You know me. I prefer the cozy ones, but I keep hearing how great these are. What's your opinion?"

"I love them, the first one more than the second, but I plowed through that one, too. They're hysterical," I said as I began to ring up his purchases.

"Excellent," he said. "And I presume you'll have her third when it comes out."

"Of course." Most customers had no idea about release dates for books, but Galen was up on all things mystery, partially because he truly loved the genre but also because he ran a very popular Instagram account for mystery enthusiasts. "After I get my morning sustenance, I'll get my #bookhaul photo of these up on Insta," he said as he headed toward the café. "I'll keep you posted on the numbers."

Galen was the universe's marketing gift to this bookstore and me. Since we opened, he has been sharing our events, posting about books he got here, and even documenting our expansion a few months back. The fact that we got orders from around the world was, I was certain, because of his attention to us as "his" bookstore.

I watched him walk over to the café with Mack following close behind. Galen was almost eighty, but he had the vim and vigor of someone much younger. And I loved that a straight, older, white guy loved cozy mysteries. He reminded me that readerships were diverse, no matter what the stereotypes said.

AT NOON, when Marcus came in, I didn't even let him reach the back room to drop off his skateboard before I said, "Car wants to give us clocks for the display. Isn't that amazing?"

Marcus smiled and said, "That is amazing." He slipped a beanie off his head and shook it a bit. "It just started to snow."

"Really?" I said and clapped my hands like a little girl as I ran toward the front of the store. Sure enough, large flakes were lilting down from the sky. It wasn't the kind of snow that would stick around, but it was beautiful nonetheless. "It's snowing," I announced to the two customers browsing the sci-fi section. They smiled politely, but clearly, they were not as excited as I was.

"So tell me about these clocks," Marcus said as he joined me by his steampunk display, where I was admiring our winter's first snow.

"Well, apparently, Car has a collection of Victorian-era

clocks. He thought they would make a good addition to the display," I said as I turned my attention to what Marcus had already set up. "It won't mess up what you had planned, will it?"

Marcus shook his head, and the tiny braids on his forehead bounced. "Not at all. I was trying to think of what props to add, and the clocks will be perfect."

"Awesome. I'll run up the street and help him carry them down if you can hold down the fort."

"Consider it held," Marcus said as he headed back to the register, where the men who had been in sci-fi were waiting with matching copies of *Neuromancer*. "Buddy read?" I heard Marcus ask the two men.

One of the guys smiled. "Actually, we're starting a sci-fi book club." He put out his hand to shake Marcus's. "We were wondering if we could hold it here."

I smiled. At this point, we had book clubs almost every night of the week in our new event and group space, and I loved it. But we didn't have any clubs run by men or that featured sci-fi. Theirs would be a good addition.

I left Marcus to it and headed out onto the street, where I stood and let the snow fall into my hair for just a bit. Then, inspired by Galen's smile from the front window of the café, I took out my phone and snapped a selfie. The flakes were lying on my red curls, and I looked Christmasy as all get out. This would make a great addition to the store's social media.

Then I headed to Car's shop and smiled when I walked in. It was warm inside and smelled of a beautiful blend of coffee and cinnamon. I wondered if Car cultivated that smell or if that was just the magical scent of his place in the world, like the scent of pine permeated my fiancé Jared's house without him having to do a thing to create it.

I heard the door chime ring in the back room, and a moment later, Car stepped out and smiled at me. "A woman of her word," he said. "I have the clocks all just here." He pointed to an array of about ten pieces on a small table near the door. "We can just cover them with these pillowcases and run them over to your shop."

"Excellent," I said. I draped the cloth over the three I thought I could handle safely and headed to my store with Car close behind. Within minutes, we had all the pieces settled onto the floor of the window display so that Marcus could do his magic.

And Marcus really did do magic. He had this sense of proportion and scale that I just didn't have, and when he designed a window display, it was guaranteed we'd sell out of most of the books he put in there.

Car and I watched Marcus work for a bit as he studied each clock and then decided, based on criteria only he knew, where to put it within the display. The two tiniest pieces were in the front with a copy of *Northern Lights* by Philip Pullman between them. It was super sweet and perfect.

Then Marcus took the largest and most ornate clock and placed it on a large box covered in black cloth. After studying the stack of books he'd pulled for a moment, he selected the four Books of Babel by Josiah Bancroft and arranged them in various states of repose on the box, too. Then, as a final touch, he spun the clock around and opened the back of it to reveal its gears.

As he did, a small piece of paper fluttered to the floor. I looked over at Car, and he stared at the paper. "Where did that come from?" he said.

"You haven't seen it before?" I asked as we both moved over to where Marcus was now holding the small, yellowed sheet.

Car shook his head. "Was that in the back of the clock?" he asked Marcus.

Marcus nodded as he handed the paper to Car, who

unfolded it and then gasped. "What is this?" He held the note out to me.

I read it and then passed it back to Marcus, who looked as befuddled as I felt. "I have no idea," Marcus said.

Written on the paper was, "He who mounts the stairs of time will find his demise."

I turned the paper over as I looked for a signature or more text. But that was it. Just that one cryptic sentence. "Is it a clue? A threat?"

Car shook his head. "I have no idea." His face was ashen, and he looked a little faint.

"Let's sit down and talk this through," I said. "Car, do you mind if I call Jared? It might just be good for the police to know about this."

Car shook his head, and Marcus draped a long arm around the small man's shoulder and helped him to the café, where Rocky quickly brought over two mugs of something that I knew would be fortifying.

I stepped into a quiet corner and dialed my fiancé. "Jared, you and Tuck free? We've got a strange situation over here at the shop."

Jared groaned because I, unfortunately, called the police with almost this exact message all too often. "Yeah, we'll be right there," he said. "You okay?"

"Totally, but I don't have a good feeling."

2

J ared and Sheriff Tucker Mason were at the shop in a matter of minutes, one of the advantages of a small town. That and the relatively low crime rate, except where I was concerned, it seemed. If people knew just how many murders I had helped solve, no one would ever come to visit, let alone live in, St. Marin's.

Fortunately, in some sort of unspoken agreement, the townies had decided not to share our crime statistics more than was legally required. The real estate agents had even found ways to spin the question about crime into some true but delightful-sounding anecdotes that included the more famous authors that had visited our store and unwillingly gotten involved in murder investigations.

So when Tuck and Jared saw the note, neither reacted with surprise. We were all far too used to strange things happening in St. Marin's. Although, this was one of the weirdest things. It actually read like a piece from a steampunk novel, which felt far too much like a portent to be only a coincidence.

The police officers read the note before pulling up chairs

and joining Car and me at the table. Marcus stayed standing so he could get into the bookstore quickly if needed.

"This was in the back of a clock?" Tuck asked. "Can I see it?" With a nod from Car, Marcus brought the clock in question back to our table. "It was this one," he said. "I opened the back to display the beautiful gears, and the paper just slid out." He caught my eye, and I nodded. He needed to get back to the store. We knew where to find him if we needed him.

"And you've never seen it?" Tuck said with a look at Car.

Car shook his head.

"When was the last time you opened the back of the clock?" Tuck asked.

Car tilted his head and looked up at the ceiling above him. "I clean all of my clocks in January, so probably then. It's been a few months." He smiled. "As you can imagine, I don't have much need to open the mechanism if the clock is working."

That made sense to me, and Tuck and Jared seemed to agree. "Where did you keep the clock?" Jared asked.

"It's been in the front window of my shop since I opened." He put his hand on the top of the timepiece. "It's a beautiful mantel clock, and while I will never sell it, I hate to be stingy and keep it to myself."

Tuck looked out the window at the street. "Is your front window like Harvey's? I mean, can people reach the display." The back of my displays was an open space, and we, or customers, could easily step in to get books if needed.

Car nodded. "Not as big, but yes. It's easy enough to reach in and get something." He looked a bit stricken as he said it. "You think someone violated my front window?"

I suppressed a chuckle at his choice of words. After all, if he felt violated, then he had been violated. And someone had, indeed, invaded space of his that they should not have. "Do you have any idea who could have done it?"

Car thought about my question for a moment and then shook his head. "I don't remember seeing anyone lingering near the window or anything." He took a deep breath. "I do keep a ledger of my customers, though, if that would be helpful. I have to break their confidence, but . . ." He looked at Tuck expectantly.

"Right now, I don't think that's necessary," Tuck said. "But thanks for letting us know. I think our best course of action is to think about the riddle and why someone might have left it for you, Mr. Radison."

"Do you have any friends or colleagues who might want to play a prank on you?" Jared asked.

"Or anyone," I said as my bookish sensibilities rose to their full height, "who might want to send you on a scavenger hunt?" I waggled my eyebrows for effect, even though I wasn't completely joking.

Car cracked a smile. "I'll have to ponder that one, but off-hand, no, I'm not exactly the pranking sort." He sighed with what seemed like regret. "Never have been, really."

Tuck nodded. "Well, please let us know if anything else unusual turns up." He handed the slip of paper to Jared. "Take a picture of this and log the case, would you?"

I so admired our sheriff. He had recently won re-election by the narrowest of margins. Yet, even in a pretty ugly election campaign that revealed some of the community's nastier attitudes toward our African American sheriff, he'd never lost focus on the core of his job—caring for the people of St. Marin's.

In the grand scheme of things, a slip of paper in the back of a clock wasn't much, a form of trespassing maybe, but Tuck knew it mattered to Car. And as I watched Jared carefully take photos of both sides of the paper, I realized Jared knew it mattered to me.

Which begged the question—why had I been so quick to

call the police? I could write that off on the fact that these men were friends, one of them my fiancé, but I knew myself better than that. Something else was at play here, and I'd learned over the past couple of years that I needed to pay attention.

Jared handed the slip of paper back to Car. "Do let us know if anything else turns up or if you think of anything that would shed some light on this." He nodded to the paper.

Car nodded. "I will. Thank you, Officers." He smiled as they hugged me, Jared adding a kiss on the cheek for good measure, and headed back out the front door.

"Shall we see what Marcus has been up to?" I said as I held my arm out for Car and led him back to the window with his clocks.

I knew I could count on Marcus to read Car's distress and to know he had a way of alleviating it a bit. And sure enough, the display was done. Marcus had finished arranging the books and printed up a small poster to set by the glass with details of the collection Car had brought over and directions to Car's shop.

As we stood behind the display, Car said, "It looks just lovely." Tears pooled in his eyes, and I pondered the older man for a moment. This was kindness, sure, but it seemed extra special to him. I wondered if being treated like part of a community was new to him.

"Let's go see it from the front," I said as I swiped a blanket from a nearby chair for each of us and wrapped one around Car's shoulders before doing the same for myself. The snow was still falling, and I was beginning to wonder if we might, indeed, have a bit of white on the ground before the day's end.

The two of us went outside, and Car's delight became even more apparent when he could see the full effect of the lights and the arrangement with the bookstore behind it. "That looks amazing."

"Just wait until we add this." My friend Cate was standing

next to us with a torso-sized object draped in black cloth. "Close your eyes. This will only take a minute."

Cate, an artist and the owner of the art co-op up the street, had been making pieces for our window displays for a long time now, but I didn't know anything about this one, so I was as excited as Car to see what she had brought.

I slipped my arm over Car's shoulders and subtly pulled him closer, sharing my body heat as I stole a bit of his. It was definitely chilly out here.

The two of us stood with our eyes closed and our bodies wrapped in a blanket as the snow fell around us. It was a lovely moment, but then a tap on the glass in front of us prompted us to open our eyes.

There, set on one side of the window, was a huge, gilded clock gear. Car gasped. "It's amazing," he said. "I wouldn't have known it, but it was just what my clocks needed, a big brother."

"Big Ben," I said with a snicker.

Car laughed hard enough to shake my arm off his shoulders. "I love that. Big Ben it is." He turned to me. "Thank you, Harvey. You have made my day."

"You're most welcome, Car. Now, let's get some more hot tea."

OFF AND ON as the day passed, I pondered the note we had found. It certainly felt ominous, but it wasn't a threat. It was too cryptic for that. But one didn't use the word *demise* casually.

Plus, it had certainly affected Car. As he left, the note in hand, he'd looked downright, not scared, but more heartbroken. I made a mental note to stop by after my shift to check on him.

As I was finishing up, Mom and Dad came in and asked if Jared and I would like to go to dinner with them over in Easton. "There's a new tapas place we thought we'd try."

"Eastern Shore tapas—sounds interesting. Let me ask Jared." I paused and said, "And would you mind if we invited another friend? He's had a bit of a day." I explained the note in Car's clock and a little about his reaction to it.

"Of course. I'll update the reservation," Dad said as he stepped away.

Mom walked with me to the register where I'd left my phone. "Tell me what the slip of paper said again?" she asked.

I looked at her with a small smile on my lips. I wasn't the only Beckett bitten by the sleuthing bug. "He who mounts the stairs of time will meet his demise," I repeated, even as I tried to turn the words and see them from new angles.

"Well, I'd be shaken up, too, if someone wrote something like that, mentioned *time*, and put it in my clock. Very ominous." Mom shivered.

I nodded. "I hadn't made the connection between time and Car's work, but you're right. Maybe we can talk with him about it a bit at dinner."

"Talk about what at dinner?" Dad said, the tilt of his head telling me he definitely suspected we were up to our investigative ways.

"I'll fill you in, dear," Mom said, "while we have lattes and wait for Harvey to check in with Jared and their new friend." She tugged him toward the café and threw a smile back at me. She loved this.

I shot a text off to Jared and then phoned Car's shop. He readily agreed to dinner, and I told him we'd stop by and get him in a few minutes. Jared replied immediately and said he'd be over shortly. We'd been having dinner together most nights as we began to plan our wedding for next fall, so tonight, we'd just have a change of venue from his house.

Jared and I had only been engaged a few months—he'd proposed on a weekend getaway to Dwayne "The Rock" Johnson's ranch over the summer—and we were taking things slow.

Neither of us were in a big rush to get married, although we were excited about it. We wanted to pay for things without going into debt, but we also wanted the day to be perfect. With Jared having never married before and it being a midlife wedding for both of us, it felt especially important to make it a great day.

Fortunately, we had the best friends in the whole world, and everyone was a part of the planning. My best friend and roommate, Mart, was my maid of honor, so she was taking care of everything from coordinating with the bridesmaids—Cate, Henri, and Elle—to catering and managing my mom, which was the biggest part of Mart's job.

Symeon, Mart's fiancé and a master chef, was going to be making all the food—bespoke brick oven pizza cooked in the brick ovens that he was getting famous for and the reason we had been at The Rock's ranch.

And the rest of our friends, including my bridesmaids' husbands Lucas and Bear, were on hand to help with anything else. The wedding was going to be at Jared's house, so he had already begun prepping the landscape, and our friends were helping haul limbs, plant shrubs, and tuck bulbs into the ground on most weekends.

I was super excited about marrying Jared, but I was almost as thrilled to have my friends involved in the process as I was to have the wedding itself. A lot had been great since I came to St. Marin's, but nothing at all compared to having the people I loved most involved in my everyday life. It was beautiful.

As promised, Jared arrived a few minutes later, and after I checked in with Marcus to be sure he didn't need me for anything else, the four of us headed over to Car's shop to pick him up.

Mom and Dad were Car's ideal customers—a little wealthy, very invested in our local community, and not afraid to show their appreciation for life's finer things. And they did just that when they walked into his small, cozy shop.

"Oh my goodness. Hank, we need this for our mantel." Mom pointed to a clock that I found to be terribly gaudy, one of those porcelain things with cherubs and a clock embedded in the center. It was, however, exactly to my mom's taste.

Dad picked up the piece and studied it intently before asking Car, who looked a bit stunned by my parents' enthusiasm. "Would you be willing to part with this?"

I smiled. Car had told me earlier today when I'd been in that, aside from his personal collection, he was happy to sell any of the clocks in the shop. "Sometimes I pick them up at auctions or estate sales, or sometimes people find the cost of repair to be too much, so I offer them a fair price for their broken timepiece and then repair them for sale in my free time."

So when Dad asked about the porcelain monstrosity, Car grinned. "Of course." They discussed the price, and before we left for dinner, Mom had a new mantel clock, and Car had made his month's rent. It was a good way to start the evening.

Unfortunately, that good start was a bit tainted when, as we walked out the door, a sour-faced woman in a parka pushed her way into the shop right through the middle of our group. When she reached Car, who was coming up behind us to lock the door, she stopped him with a hand to his chest.

"Car Radison, we need to talk," she spat at him.

Car looked startled and shot me a quick glance. "Mildred, this will have to wait. I'm about to go out to dinner with friends." His words were firm, but his voice was soft.

Mildred threw back her faux-fur-lined hood. "Dinner will have to wait." Then she turned to us and, in a much softer but absolutely grating tone, said, "I do apologize, but I need Car this evening."

I looked at Car, and his eyes were wide with what seemed to be fear. "I'm sorry, but did you not hear Car say he had plans? Is someone bleeding?" I asked, quoting what my mother said when I'd interrupted her as a child.

"What?" the woman said. "No, no one is bleeding." She looked at Car as he began to move toward the door again. "Where are you going?"

"I told you, Mildred. I have plans. Come by in the morning, and we can talk then."

My dad—a large man who, while gentlemanly, hated bullies as much as I did—put his hand on Mildred's shoulder and moved her toward the door in front of him. "It's been nice to meet you," he said as he nearly shoved her back into the cold.

Outside, now with the door shut behind her, Mildred was throwing an all-out temper tantrum, foot stomping, swearing, and all.

But Car was smiling. "Shall we go out the back door?" he said.

After leaving through the alley door of Car's shop, we all walked around the block to where Mom and Dad had parked their Tesla SUV. It had been Dad's dream to own a Tesla for years, and now that we had charging stations at the Maritime Museum, something Dad and the museum director Lucas had worked hard for, he had splurged. It was a beautiful car, with room enough for five passengers, and being a four-wheel-drive, it was the perfect car for tonight's snowy ride to the nearest city.

Once we had double-checked to be sure that Mildred hadn't thrown a brick through Car's window and Jared had let Tuck know about the grumpy woman on the sidewalk, we settled in for the beautiful ride to Easton.

The Eastern Shore doesn't get much snow, which was one of the few things I didn't like about living here, but today, it was an actual storm, and I could see the snow settling in the grass and along the colder strips of pavement. We might just have a snow day tomorrow. On the ride to the restaurant, we made small talk about the town and the upcoming holiday bazaar. Car was planning on doing free battery replacements for watches, which I thought was a genius idea. He beamed when I told him so. "This event is going to be amazing," I said, and I genuinely thought so.

At the restaurant, the host took us to a lovely table by the window, and I was glad to be able to keep watching it snow, mostly for the beauty but also because I didn't want Dad to test his new wheels too much.

With our orders placed and our drinks delivered, I broached the subject of the grumpy woman in the parka. "So, Car, forgive me for being nosy, but who was that Mildred woman?"

Jared actually snickered under his breath when I admitted I was being nosy because everyone in St. Marin's knew I could not bear to be left out of any of the scandals around town. I always said I preferred to think of myself as curious, but nosy was a fairly accurate term.

Car sighed and sipped his hot tea before saying, "Mildred is my sister. My busy-body bossy sister." He shook his head. "I do love her, but she is a pain in the rear."

I laughed and almost spat my soda across the table.

"She did seem a bit, um, forceful," Mom said. "Any idea what she wanted?"

Clearly, the nosiness tendency was genetic. I saw my dad and Jared exchange a look. At least they were connecting over the nosiness of the women they loved.

"She followed me down here from Boston and said she

needed to keep an eye on me. Now, she thinks the shop is too much, that I should sell and retire." He closed his eyes. "The worst thing I can think of is retirement, just sitting around all day, watching TV and puttering."

"I hear you there," Dad said. He'd retired a bit ago, but then he'd started a new consulting business in St. Marin's. He wasn't great at sitting around and puttering, either.

I studied Car's face for a minute, trying to decide if I could really be this nosy. I decided I could be and asked my question. "Why does she think you can't handle it?"

Car smiled. "Older sisters are protective by nature, I think," he said. "But mine has more reason than most to be. I haven't always been healthy."

I nodded. "I see. So, she's worried you're pushing yourself too hard."

"Exactly," Car said. "What she doesn't understand is that working is part of what helps me stay well." He looked at the four of us at the table. "I have bipolar disorder, and while I have been quite well for years now, and my family doesn't know my actual diagnosis, Mildred is always afraid."

"Oh, that's a serious illness," Jared said, "but I'm glad to hear you're well now. That's great."

"It is great," Car said. "I just wish Mildred could accept that I don't need her tending me anymore."

We let the weight of that wish sit with us for a bit before Jared deftly changed the subject and asked about Mom's charity work. Mom could talk for hours—and did—about the work she did in the community. Fortunately, despite her deep personal involvement in several important charities, she was far more invested in the work these organizations did for our community than in what she did for them.

She filled us in on the Literacy Council's latest activities and then shared how the Chamber of Commerce was going to provide free hot chocolate for the bazaar next weekend. I've known my mom, well, my whole life, though, so despite her breezy conversation, I could tell she was building to something. Apparently, Dad could, too, because he bumped his leg against mine under the table when Mom said, "Actually, Car, I could use your opinion."

Here we go, I thought.

"One thing the bazaar next weekend doesn't have is a fundraising element. I've recently joined the board of the Mental Health Association." She paused and looked at Car thoughtfully. "If you might be interested, perhaps you'd like to help me coordinate something."

Car beamed. "I'd love to help." He paused. "But on one condition. We have to include an educational element in whatever we do. People are frightened by people with mental illness, so there's little sympathy, which I'd like to change."

"Me, too," Mom said and squeezed Car's hand on the table. "Can I come by tomorrow so we can begin planning?"

"Perfect," Car said.

THE REST of the evening was absolutely delightful, and the ride back was only slightly adventurous as Dad learned to navigate his new hundred and fifty K car in the snow. "Where should I drop you, Car?" Dad asked as we came back into town.

Car smiled. "At the shop." He blushed. "I know it's a little Dickensian," he said, "but I live in the apartment upstairs."

"I love it," I said. "Those apartments are so cute. And now that I know that, when we have extra pastries in the café, maybe Rocky can bring them to you." I didn't doubt that Car had enough income to live on, but I couldn't imagine a small-town clock shop could give him a lot of extra cash.

"Always," he said as Dad pulled up behind the shop.

Jared hopped out and walked with Car to the door. It was

slick out there, and none of us wanted anyone to fall and get hurt.

Car unlocked the back door, and as he opened it, he jumped back.

There, at his feet, lay the parka-clad body of his sister, Mildred.

3

As the coroner took away Mildred's body, Mom and I sat with Car in his quaint apartment and sipped more tea. I totally understood why the British relied on the beverage so much. It was very, very soothing.

Car was quite upset, of course, and Mom and I had thought it best to stay with him while Dad went to my house to feed and walk the dogs since Mart was out late at a winery event for her job that evening. Car wasn't saying much, but he had stopped crying. Mostly, he was sipping his tea and watching the snow that continued to fall. I wondered if the snowflakes gave him as much comfort as they gave me at that moment.

"Harvey, might I make a recommendation for your bookstore?" Car asked.

When I nodded but looked a bit puzzled, he said, "I asked Mildred to read it just after I found it because it's a powerful look at how my illness works. I wanted her to understand, not just hear the name of the illness. But she never would. I thought maybe if your store carried it..." His voice trailed off as he looked back at the snow.

"Absolutely, Car. What's the book?" I asked as I put my hand on his arm.

"*A Star Called Bitterness* by Trevor McCall." He looked over at me and nodded as I typed the title and author's name into my phone.

"I'll order it first thing tomorrow," I said.

"Thank you," he said. "I do wish Mildred had read it."

I nodded. "I'm so sorry," I said for about the thirtieth time. "I know you'll miss her."

Car smiled. "I will, pain in the butt that she was. I wonder if she was here waiting for me."

"Did she have a key to the building?" Mom asked. "Maybe she let herself in to get out of the cold while she waited."

Car shook his head. "No. She had asked for one, but I needed to keep that boundary firm. I loved having her close by, but I also needed my personal space."

It was the exact same reason I hadn't given my parents a key to my shop. They had one to Mart's house, just as back up, but my store was my sacred space, and while I knew they respected that, I needed to have the boundary clear in my mind, too.

But if Mildred didn't have a key, how had she gotten in? I thought the question at Mom, and she nodded as if my telepathic signal had gotten through loud and clear. Something weird was going on.

Tuck and Jared came up the stairs that began near the back door of Car's shop and ended in his studio apartment. "Nothing seems to be disturbed in the shop," Jared said. "But let us know if you find something out of place."

"How are you doing?" Tuck said as he pulled up a chair and sat next to Car.

"As well as can be expected," Car said. "Thank you all for your kindness."

Jared sat down next to me on the small settee in the corner. "Of course," he said. "Is there anything you need?"

Car shook his head. "To be honest, I think I'd just like to read for a while and then go to sleep."

We all stood. Mom gave Car a hug, and then we made our way back downstairs and out the door. The walk to my shop was longer than usual simply because we had to negotiate the snow that had begun to accumulate, but still, none of us talked. It seemed like we'd all agreed to some thinking time.

But when we got to the bookstore, where our newest clerk Maybelle was beginning to close up for the night, everything spilled out of us. At the same time.

Mom said, "Poor Car."

Jared said, "So odd that she was inside the building."

I said, "I'm so tired of finding dead bodies."

But Tuck's voice was the loudest, at least figuratively speaking. "Mildred Radison was murdered."

"Did you say that woman was murdered?" my dad said as he helped Maybelle bring over mugs of decaf for each of us. "Really?"

Tuck nodded as he sipped his coffee. "Strangled. I can't be absolutely certain until the autopsy, but the finger marks on her neck were a pretty good indicator."

I sighed. Another murder. Another murder I wouldn't be able to stay away from trying to solve. I knew Tuck was only telling us this information because we'd been there. Well, and because I'd pry it out of him later anyway. I had a sort of reputation for these things.

"At least we know Car didn't do it," Mom said.

"He was with you the entire night?" Tuck asked.

"Yep, and we saw his sister very much alive just before we left. There is absolutely no way he killed her." A tiny dance of relief moved through my chest. I was tired of my friends, even my new friends, being charged with murder.

"How can we help, Tuck?" my dad asked.

Tuck, to his credit, managed to only smile and shook his

head at the question. "In normal towns, civilians don't help the police investigate murders."

I sighed. "In normal towns, someone isn't killed every three months." I wanted to add, *In normal towns, the bookstore owner and her friends don't stumble across every dead body,* but I kept that uncomfortable observation to myself.

Jared took my hand and then looked at Tuck. "How about, Sheriff, you and I discuss what Harvey and crew need to know each day, and then I can relay the appropriate information?" He turned back to me. "That way, you can be sure we're telling you all we think is appropriate and save yourself the worry of trying to figure out more than you should." I could see the hope in his eyes at his suggestion. He hated my sleuthing almost more than Tuck, which was saying something.

"I like that plan," Tuck said. "In the meantime, you know the protocol here. No talking about this with anyone." He tapped the table twice and stood up with his mug before carrying it to the sink behind the café counter, washing it, and setting it facedown to dry.

The rest of us followed suit, and then Mom, Dad, and Tuck headed home for the night. Jared and I stayed to help Maybelle and Marcus close up. It felt weird to leave my store when things needed to be done, and I wanted to let Marcus know what had happened. He didn't count as "anyone" when it came to this stuff, and both the police and I knew that.

After I told Marcus what happened, he said, "Older white woman. Big coat with a hood."

"Yep, regular old Nanook of the north," I said. "You saw her?"

"She came in just after you left, got a coffee, and then browsed for a while. I ended up selling her a copy of *An Unquiet Mind*," Marcus said as he logged out of the register.

"Well, that's interesting. Maybe she had actually begun to understand her brother a bit?" I mused.

"Car has bipolar disorder?" Marcus asked as we gathered Maybelle and Jared and headed toward the front door. I nodded, not wanting to say more in front of Maybelle. She was new enough to the store that talking about murder might scare her off. Plus, she hadn't yet earned her credentials for our Sleuthing Squad, as Jared sometimes called us.

With words of caution for everyone as they headed home—fortunately, all of us were walking—Jared and I turned up the street toward our houses.

"Where to, m'lady?" Jared said as he slipped my hand into the crook of his arm.

"My house, if you don't mind. I miss the dogs." I sighed. "And Aslan."

"You know it's been a long day when you miss that grumpy girl," Jared said as he pulled me a bit closer.

He was right. I adored my fat, lazy cat, but she was independent, only choosing to snuggle when it suited her. My dogs were my go-to comfort companions. Even Sasquatch, with all his wiggles, was more prone to settle in for an evening of TV and blankets than my cat. Still, I loved her, and I knew she loved me . . . in her own way.

We slowly made our way along the snow-covered sidewalks, and I tried to keep myself in the present moment by admiring the much smaller flakes that were falling now and the way white dusted the trees. It really was a lovely evening, and the walk did much to soothe my nerves.

When we got home, the house was still dark, which meant Mart hadn't made it back from her work event yet. As soon as we got inside, I texted her to see if she was okay.

Staying here for the night. The roads are a little too treacherous for this California girl, and I have to be back at eight a.m., anyway, she replied back.

They have a bed for you?

I could almost hear my best friend's exasperation. *It's a*

massive bed and breakfast, Harvey. I have my choice of luxury
bedrooms with ensuites.

I laughed at her response. *Enjoy your overnight vacation,* I
texted back. *I'll catch you up on the latest in the morning.*

Sounds good. You didn't find another dead body, did you?

I sent her the laughing emoji. No need to ruin her relaxing
night at her employer's newest business acquisition, The
Woodlawn. I'd let Mart enjoy the time away before I told her
how right she was.

WHEN I WOKE up stupidly early the next morning, I decided to
make Jared and me scrambled eggs and bacon because I could
feel the familiar knot in my chest that meant my body was
aware of something I hadn't come to understand yet, and the
best way I knew to reconcile my mind and my somatic systems
was to do something else for a while to see what surfaced. So, I
made coffee and set out the food to make breakfast when I
heard Jared beginning to stir. And then I settled into my
reading chair with my latest book, *Chapter and Curse* by Elizabeth Penney, a bookstore mystery set in Cambridge, England. It
was a delight.

I was reading along, thoroughly enjoying the book chatter
and the sleuth Molly's ability to be in just the right place at the
right time, when I came to the mention of a note stuck to their
shop door. My heart danced a bit, and I put the book down.

With my eyes closed, I turned my mind toward the center of
my chest, where I felt the twinge, and waited. And like a photograph, there was an image of the note Marcus had found in the
back of Car's clock.

My eyes flew open. I picked up my coffee mug for forti-
fication.

I grabbed my laptop and typed in the cryptic verse from the
note. Nothing. It wasn't a quote from anything—at least, not

something well-known enough to be on the Internet. So not a quote, in all likelihood. It must have been written specifically for Car, then. But why?

The words read like a warning more than a threat, although I wasn't sure the distinction between those two things was really that great now that I thought about it. If the person penning the note was also the person who might bring about the demise, that was definitely a threat, not just a warning.

But if the person who wrote it knew about something and wanted to keep Car safe, then we were looking for a friend, not a foe. Still, that friend had to know something that might be crucial for Car, so if they really were a friend, wouldn't they just tell him?

I heard the shower turn on, so I walked to the kitchen, poured myself more coffee, and put on the bacon. I couldn't get any further with my thought process without more information, and since I didn't know how to get more information yet, I needed to put my ideas aside.

Remembering a session with a great counselor from a couple of years back, I pulled forth the image of a music box that had been my grandmother's, and as I beat the eggs to a froth, I imagined putting the ideas about Mildred's murder and the note inside the music box and locking it. They'd be there when I was ready to return to them, but for now, they were safe and handled.

It was a small mental exercise, but I'd been using it often these days when I found myself sliding into worry about the wedding or finances for the bookstore during times I could do nothing about either of them. Just having a space to sequester those thoughts mentally was immensely helpful.

As the bacon sizzled on the griddle, I poured the eggs into a generous portion of melted butter and watched them begin to solidify. It was almost magical the way heat changed food. I flipped the bacon, stirred the eggs, and returned to my book with my coffee. It was a good morning, I decided.

WITH OUR BELLIES nice and full, Jared and I walked the three dogs to the bookstore around nine. Sasquatch led the way with his tiny legs, and I wondered if he knew he was going home this afternoon. Cate had been working on a major photography project that was, she said, taking up their entire living room floor, and Sasquatch could not be trusted with photos.

"I think he likes the taste of the chemicals or something," Cate had told me. "He licks the images right off the paper."

"Oh my. That can't be good for him, can it?" I'd asked.

"He's still alive and kicking, so I guess it's okay. But it's definitely not okay for my photographs, and these are old ones, which were found in a box in someone's attic a few months ago, and can't be reprinted," Cate had said.

So it was that Sasquatch had been Mayhem and Taco's roomie for the past week. But Cate was hanging her installation at the co-op today, so Sasquatch could return to his only dog status in a few hours. I was pretty sure he was looking forward to that. My dogs were friendly but also attention-hogs. Sasquatch was certainly not getting all the loving to which he was typically accustomed.

When we arrived at the shop, I was surprised to see Marcus already there. He wasn't due to come in until noon. "What brought you in early?"

"A dream-inspired idea," he said from the front window. "Look what I've found."

Jared and I moved over and looked at what he held—five more pieces of paper.

"More notes? You found these in the clocks?" I asked.

Marcus nodded. "I think we can be certain they're clues now. I have no idea to what, but there's a pattern." He stepped down from the window and led us to the register counter. "See?"

He set four more pieces of paper in a line on the counter. Slowly, I read through each cryptic note, getting the clear sense that this was a riddle or puzzle of some sort. In equal measure, though, I got more confused as I read.

THE STITCH *in time never saves nine or ten.*
Time's hands never move unless prodded with invisibility.
Abide with me, and I'll abide with time.
Time is never up . . . until it is.

I SHOOK MY HEAD. "Obviously, these notes are for Car." I tapped the word *time* on each note. "But I have no idea what they mean except that they totally creep me out."

Marcus sighed. "Me, too. Jilted lover, maybe?"

I stared at the clues again and looked over at Jared. "I expect you'll want these?"

He nodded. "And I'll need to dust the clocks. I know you've all been touching them, but given that these could be linked to a murder case, we need to be very thorough."

Marcus headed toward the window to remove the clocks with a soft cloth.

I leaned against Jared and closed my eyes. "I'm not sure I'm up for this," I said.

Jared rubbed my shoulders. "You know what's good about that? You don't have to be up for anything." He turned me toward him. "I know you're curious, Harvey. I also know Car is your friend, and you want to help him. But why not let us handle this one? Just sit this one out."

From somewhere deep inside my chest, a soft assent rang out. "Okay," I said. "Thank you."

Jared stared at me for a minute, and while he might have made a joke at a lighter moment, he seemed to understand that I needed something different. "Good," he said as he kissed my forehead. "I'll still keep you updated as I can, but we've got this, Harvey. You enjoy the holidays."

I looked outside at the shimmer of snow still tucked into the corners of the grass and street. "I will," I said, committing to that affirmation for myself. *This was going to be the best Christmas ever*, I thought as I turned from Jared with a giggle. I felt lighter already.

Jared packed up the clocks and said he'd get them back to us as soon as possible, then kissed my cheek and headed out to his truck, which was still parked on the street from last night.

We had a small problem for the shop now that Jared had taken Car's clocks into evidence. We had to fill out the display somehow. I was just walking over to the window to talk with Marcus about that when I saw a small woman with jet-black hair approaching our front door.

Normally, I let early customers read our hours posted on the door, but today, I felt festive. I opened the door and said, "Happy Holidays. I'm sorry, but we don't open for another little bit." I smiled.

The woman looked up at me and said, "I understand. I was going to see my friend Carson Radison at his shop, but it appears he isn't open yet either." She glanced up the street toward Car's shop. "Is there anywhere warm I can sit until he opens?"

It was still quite cold, and the woman had on ballet slippers that looked like they were already soaked through. "You know what, come on in. The café will have coffee soon, and you can sit there to stay warm until we open."

She smiled, and her face softened noticeably. "I'm Komiko," she said as she stepped into the door and basked in the heat. "Thank you."

"No problem," I said. "I'm Harvey, and this is my store." I walked her over to the café, where Rocky was setting out the morning's first carafes of coffee. "Rocky, meet Komiko. She's a friend of Car's."

Rocky smiled. "Excellent. Coffee?"

"Yes, please," Komiko said, and I waved as I left Rocky to serve our guest. I still needed to figure out a solution to our window problem.

But, of course, I didn't need to worry. Marcus had already pulled some art and photography books that featured images of clocks and added them to the display, with each book propped open to a fitting image. It wasn't as striking as the clocks themselves, but the theme was still conveyed. Plus, now we had more books on display, and high-dollar ones, too.

As I finished up my opening routine, I thought about calling Jared and telling him a friend of Car's was in my store, but then I decided I knew nothing about this woman, that she could be here on this ill-fated week by coincidence, and that, most importantly, I didn't have to work this case.

I hadn't convinced myself completely yet, but I'd learned in the past few months that beliefs are just things we tell ourselves until we believe them. I'd just have to keep convincing myself.

THE STORE WAS UNUSUALLY busy when we opened, and I realized school was closed for the day. School always closed here if there was even a hint of snow, even a prediction. But the roads were completely fine, so teenagers and parents with young children were looking for a way to spend the extra time. In a small town like ours, the local bookstore was always a good bet, especially since today was story day.

A quick scan of the ages of the children in the shop at eleven told me I needed to broaden my selection of titles for storytime to give the elementary-age kids something to enjoy.

So, in addition to *A Unicorn Named Sparkle's First Christmas*, I selected *Most Marshmallows* by Rowboat Watkins because I loved his books, and I thought the older kids might enjoy the inspiring story.

Storytime was a huge success, and we sold all the copies we had of Sparkle's book, so we put orders in for several more of those as well as Watkins' title. Plus, I knew our general children's revenue would be up because we sold a bunch more books, too, as parents, grandparents, and other caregivers stocked up for holiday gifts.

And, of course, the holiday season meant everyone wanted hot cocoa with a candy cane stirrer, so Rocky's café was hopping, too. Everywhere in our little part of the world felt festive, and I loved it.

What I didn't love was that Komiko was still sitting in the café. I mean, I didn't mind that she was hanging out there, but I was concerned that she hadn't yet connected with Car. "Komiko, no word from Car yet?"

She shook her head. "I've called his shop several times, but he hasn't answered. I hope he's okay."

I sat down with her and struggled with what to tell her about his personal life, specifically Mildred. I decided I could only make that decision with a bit more information. "Have you guys known each other a long time?" I asked.

Komiko smiled. "A few years. We met a bit ago when we stayed at the same place." She smiled. "We've kept in touch since."

"Well, I know Car had a family crisis last night, but I saw him then. He was upset but okay." I didn't feel comfortable revealing more to this woman I'd just met, but if they had been friends a while, I figured he'd want her to know that he'd had a hard week. "Do you want to walk over there and see if we can find him? He lives above the shop, so maybe he's just taking the day off."

She smiled. "That would be great. I didn't want to seem creepy or like a stalker or something, but I am concerned." She looked at me carefully. "Especially since he had a blow yesterday." There was weight to her words that I didn't fully understand, but I knew genuine care when I saw it. Komiko cared about Car.

It was time for Marcus's shift to start formally, and I typically took my lunch now anyway. So I told Marcus I was going to step out but that I'd be back in a bit. Then he could take an extended break since he'd come in so early.

He smiled and shook his head. He wouldn't take an extra break. I knew him too well for that. But of course, I probably wouldn't do the same in his position. We both loved our jobs so much. Every day, I marveled at how lucky I was to work with books all day, and I knew Marcus felt the same way.

I grabbed my coat and scarf and bundled up as Komiko put on her thin jacket. That pink thing didn't look warm enough to do any good at all. Between that and her shoes, no wonder she had wanted to get out of the cold. I was glad it was just a quick walk to Car's shop.

When we got there, the store was dark, and I could see from the single light that Car left on near the back that he wasn't in there. But given that I now knew he lived upstairs, I thought it likely I might find a bell for his apartment if I looked. Sure enough, tucked into the space between the shop's doorframe and the brick of the entrance alcove was a small black button. I pressed it and heard an old-fashioned telephone bell ring from above.

I stepped out onto the street and looked up at Car's windows. He peered through the curtains, saw me, and held up one finger. A moment later, he was unlocking the front door to greet me.

His greeting faltered quite a bit when he saw Komiko standing next to me. "What are *you* doing here?"

4

I immediately regretted telling Komiko where Car lived
and started to apologize, but before I could get a word in,
Car said, "Well, you've found me now. Come in."

I looked over at Komiko, who looked a bit embarrassed but
also relieved, and the two of us followed Car through the shop
and up the stairs to his apartment. Once inside, the three of us
sat in his little sitting area by the windows and stared at one
another.

Finally, I broke the silence by saying, "Car, Komiko came
into my shop to get out of the cold while she waited for your
store to open. She was concerned about you."

His voice softened. "You've been waiting?" he said.

She nodded quickly. "I moved to Baltimore recently, and I
knew from our last email exchange that you'd moved out to St.
Marin's." She blushed. "I hope it's okay that I came by."

Car smiled gently. "I'm sorry for my reaction before. I've
had a difficult couple of days, and sometimes, well,
sometimes—"

"Sometimes, I bring even more difficulty. I know." She

sighed. "But I'm doing a lot better now. I'm feeling good. Working full-time. Have my own place."

I quietly stood and went into Car's kitchen since I wanted to give the old friends some privacy, or as much as was possible in a studio apartment, and because I figured Car wouldn't mind if I made us all some tea. I put on the electric kettle and was grateful its gentle hum drowned out most of what Car and Komiko were saying.

A few moments later, I carried a small tray I'd found beside the stove over to the table by the window and set out the kettle, tea bags, three mugs, and some milk and sugar I'd rummaged out of Car's cabinets. I grinned with embarrassment as I sat down next to Car. "I kind of made myself at home," I said.

Car patted my hand. "I'm very glad you did," he said. "Friends who feel comfortable in my home are the best kind." He picked up a mug, put in a teabag, added hot water, and then passed the kettle to Komiko so she could do the same.

"Car told me that you know about his illness, Harvey, so now I can tell you a bit more about how we met," Komiko said as she fixed her tea. "If that's okay with you, Car?"

"Of course," he said. "Komiko and I stayed at the same hospital for a while to get the medical care we needed."

"I have depression," she said. "A pretty severe case, and it was really bad for a while. I had to be taken into the hospital to protect me."

"Oh, I'm so sorry. Depression is so awful. I've struggled with it myself, although a milder form than you—at least so far—so I can sort of imagine." It was only recently that I had come to terms with my own mental illness, recognizing that my brain just didn't regulate my mood the way it was designed to. Therapy, meditation, and medication helped, though, and I was grateful for all of them.

Komiko nodded. "You do know, then. And Car was a big part of my healing process."

"Thank you, dear girl. I'm so glad you're doing better. So glad." I could definitely see Car's affection for her. It was fatherly and protective but also not completely open. I got the sense that he had helped her far more than she had helped him, especially given how he had greeted her earlier.

I wondered briefly if his hesitations were due to Komiko's illness. Loving someone very sick was always hard, I imagined, but a mental illness seemed even harder since mental health wasn't something our society took very seriously. It seemed that Car had carried more than his fair share of the mental health burden.

Komiko stood and put on her thin jacket. "Well, I'm going to go. I'm staying in Easton for a few days and will enjoy the holiday spirit out of the city for a bit. Maybe we can get dinner before I go?" she asked Car.

"I would like that," Car said.

I noticed he didn't go far enough in that expression to set a date, but how he handled his social life was his affair. "Thanks for having us, Car."

"Actually, Harvey, would you mind walking Komiko down and then stopping back up for a minute? I have to ask you a business-related question." He smiled at me.

"Sure. I'll be right back." I followed Komiko down the stairs and said goodbye before locking the shop's front door and heading back upstairs to Car's rooms.

Car was sitting in the same chair, but he was stretched out now, his feet on a low stool to the side of the table. When he heard me come in, he looked toward the door. "Thanks for coming back up, Harvey. I won't keep you long."

"I've got all the time you need, Car. What's up? You said a business question?"

"Well, that was sort of a fib. I didn't want to make Komiko feel bad, you see." He took a deep breath. "She is a lovely woman with a terrible illness, but she's also a bit of a gossip, so

I've learned to hold my cards close to my vest with her if you will."

I nodded. In my life, I'd had a few friends I loved but could not trust with my most personal or painful stories because they simply didn't seem to give me the support I needed. Or, in one really bizarre situation, a friend from college had turned the story of my painful divorce into a podcast episode to talk about "rock bottoms." The episode itself might have been okay, but she used my name. We haven't spoken since.

"Understood completely," I said to Car. "Something about Mildred?"

"Maybe," he said as he rubbed a small spot on his left arm. "I spoke with Sheriff Mason this morning, and he told me about the other notes Marcus found. He said they were checking the clocks carefully for evidence."

I nodded. "I'm glad they called you. What did you think of the notes?"

"They sent me pictures." Car held up his phone. "But I can't make hide nor hair of them. That's what I wanted to ask you. When you read them, did you have any insights?"

Inwardly, I groaned. I was being pulled into this investigation even though I was trying hard not to be, but Car was my friend, and I certainly wasn't going to put my desire to just enjoy the holidays over his grief and the strange violations we'd found in his clocks. After all, our use of his clocks brought the notes to light in the first place.

"Unfortunately, no. I guess they were all related to time," I said with a shrug. "But beyond that, I'm afraid I'm not much help."

Car nodded. "Same here. Well, if you think of anything, you'll let me know?"

"I will," I said. "I'll ponder it a bit and get back to you if anything comes to me." I stood up. "Do you need anything? Groceries? Dinner?"

"No. Thank you, though. I'll venture out later today and get out into the crisp air. It'll do me good." He stood beside me. "Maybe I'll venture into your shop and pick up something entertaining to read."

We walked to the apartment door together. "Do that. I'll be there until about five, but Marcus will be in until ten. Either of us can make recommendations."

"Perfect," he said. "Oh, may I ask one other favor?"

"Anything," I said.

"My sister's service will be on Saturday. Could I ask you to come?" His brow furrowed with sadness.

"Of course. I will be there, and I'm sure Mom and Dad would like to come, too." I leaned forward and hugged him. "Could we do a little reception for you in my store after? Just some light food and coffee."

He smiled. "That would be lovely. Thank you."

I hugged him again and then went down the stairs. I was starving, and to my delight, Lu's taco truck was on the street. Plus, I needed to ask her if she'd cater a small reception on Saturday.

Lu Mason was the sheriff's wife, but more importantly, she owned the best food truck in Maryland. Her mole sauce was world-renowned, if only because I insisted that everyone who asked for a restaurant recommendation in the bookstore try it.

When Lu opened the window of her truck, the steam from inside billowed out, and suddenly, the air was fragrant with spice and cooking meat. My stomach growled so hard that I felt it against my ribcage. "Thank goodness, Lu," I said. "I am starving."

"Apparently," she said with a laugh. "Pork with mole is especially good today," she said.

"I'll take two tacos, please." I handed her my cash—which she tried to turn away, as usual, and only took when I insisted.

"Seriously, Lu, if none of us paid each other in this town, we'd all go bankrupt."

"Maybe we just need to set up a commune and barter," she said with a smile. "We're just passing the same money back and forth all the time."

"I'm hoping our cash is like the Delorian, and it builds energy as it gets up to speed," I said with a chuckle.

"Marty McFly for the win," Lu said as she handed me my tacos.

I asked her about catering the reception for Car on Saturday, and she readily agreed. "Tuck told me about his sister. How awful."

I nodded. "I just came from seeing Car. He's okay, but what a blow. And for an older single man with no other family, it has to be especially hard."

"Oh, Tuck said he had another sister. You didn't know?" Lu said.

I shook my head. "No, he hasn't mentioned her, but I don't know him that well." I was a bit puzzled by this lack of knowledge. Maybe Car and his other sister weren't close, which was why he hadn't mentioned her to me. "Is she coming into town for the funeral?"

"Tuck called her. That's all I know. Said the woman was kind of brusque." She shook her head. "It takes all kinds."

I nodded. That was a refrain I repeated to myself often when I met people who rubbed me the wrong way. I didn't know most of the details of anyone's story, so I couldn't judge why they were the way they were.

"Thanks, Lu," I said as I waved a taco in the air and headed back to the shop.

I was hungry enough to inhale both tacos in the short walk back. They were so good, and I could have eaten two more. But I knew that in a few minutes, I'd feel full and regret that overindulgence if I took it. Instead, I decided to treat myself to something sugary from Rocky's café later.

The store was a bit quieter than it had been this morning. I assumed the children and their caregivers had returned to their homes to watch movies, take naps, or such. At least, that was what I'd always done with Mom on snow days when I was a kid.

But we still had a few customers. Two teenage girls sat near the YA section with the full set of Sabaa Tahir's Ember in the Ashes quartet. They had cash in their hands and kept looking at the back of the books and then recounting their money. I had been in that position many a time, and it was one of the best things about owning my own bookstore that I could help facilitate access to books.

"Women," I said as I stopped behind their chairs. "Did you know there's a special on that set today? Each book is twenty-five percent off." I hoped that was a big enough discount to allow them to buy the books. I wanted to help them, not insult them.

Their faces lit up, and as I walked away, I saw them recounting and then heard the squeals as they must have figured out they could get all four books. Ah, my day was made. Marcus was busy straightening the self-help section, and I moseyed over to see what he was up to. Whatever it was, he was hindered quite a bit in his efforts by the presence of three prone dogs at his feet.

"You have company, I see," I said when I reached him. "Supervisors."

"Sleeping on the job," he said as he stepped over the basset hound. "Why do we have dog beds for them again?"

"I ask myself that question daily," I said with a laugh. "Anything new that looks good?"

Marcus held up a book. "Not new, but I've been meaning to

read this. Have you?" He held up a copy of James Clear's *Atomic Habits*.

"Oh yeah. I read it when I opened the store. Really good stuff." I studied the classy cover with the gold shimmer. "You feeling like you need to get some things nailed down?"

He smiled at me. "Well, I'm writing a novel—"

I interrupted him before he could say more. "What? You are? That's amazing. Tell me all about it." I paused. "That is if you're talking about it. Maybe you're not talking about it. Sorry." I was rambling, and I knew it, but I was just so excited. Marcus had the best mind for stories I'd ever seen, and that he might apply that knowledge and love to his own book was beyond exciting.

He shook his head. "I'm not talking about it yet. Storing up the energy in it, so to speak, but I hope you'll beta read it for me when it's done."

I jumped up and down carefully so as not to squish any pooches. "Are you kidding me? Of course. I'd be honored. Wow."

He set Clear's book aside and said, "Okay, time for me to extricate myself from the canine wilderness and get some lunch. I saw Lu outside."

"Pork and mole today. Trust me," I said as I watched him place his giant feet carefully between the twelve paws wrapped around each other on the floor. "You should probably look into diamond heists. You'd be a master with the lasers." I laughed as he did a cartwheel toward the door. I wasn't wrong.

THE AFTERNOON WAS steady with customers, which I didn't take for granted in the off-season here in St. Marin's. Even in the few years since I've been in town, I'd seen some businesses start strong with the tourist season only to falter and fail when the colder months hit. Those of us who survived this boom-bust cycle did so because we planned ahead financially and did all we could to drive traffic for all of us during the holidays. If we could make a good profit margin during December, we could usually ride out the quiet time of January through March.

Hence, the holiday bazaar. We'd pooled resources as business owners to get the word out, and the Chamber had done a lot of advertising too. Everyone hoped this would be the first year of an annual tradition that gave all of us a little breathing room come the new year.

In fact, I needed to get going on our sale plans for the bazaar. We were going to be launching our new membership club during the event, and while I had ordered the brochures and membership cards a while back, I hadn't yet decided what the exact structure of the program would be.

So while Marcus managed the store, I set myself up in the back room with my giant whiteboard, the materials, and a whole bunch of colorful dry-erase markers. Colors and whiteboards made everything easier to plan, I'd found. Plus, they took me back to my school days and chalkboards. I loved those messy things.

But even with the fun "school supplies," I was having trouble focusing on my task at hand, given that this whiteboard had, in the past, doubled as my very own "murder board," just like they created in police shows. I had to fight every temptation to flip it over and begin scribbling notes about Mildred's murder.

Fortunately, I was saved from myself by the arrival of two of my closest friends, Stephen and Walter. The couple were such fixtures at the store that they walked into the back room as if they worked there, which they sometimes did, but only on a volunteer basis.

"What is happening back here?" Walter said as he looked at the bright-red cards and brochures strewn across the table and then at the mostly blank whiteboard onto which I'd only managed to scribble, "Membership Club."

I sat down heavily. "I'm trying to devise a plan, and I'm distracted."

Stephen sat down beside me. "Want to talk about it?"

I did, of course, but I also knew that talking about it would only make me begin to theorize. And I wasn't going to do that, not this time.

"Is it about that woman's murder?" Walter asked as he straightened the table and began to read the brochure.

He was acting nonchalant, but I knew these men. They were as curious as I was. I also knew, though, that they would respect my wishes. "I can't talk about it, guys. I promised Jared I would stay out of things, and I'm committed to that promise." Even as I said it, I confirmed to myself it was still true. I really didn't want to actively try to solve another murder.

"What I want to do," I said as I stood back up, "is figure out how to turn this membership program into something customers love that will drive our profits. Want to help?"

Stephen and Walter Arritt-Hitchcock were both successful businessmen, and Walter's contracting business here in St. Marin's had taken off. They knew how to turn a profit.

"You got it," Stephen said as he handed me a blue marker and took an orange one for himself. "Love, tell us what we've got."

For the next hour, the three of us took my thin outline of the program from my brochure and fleshed it out into a profit-driving, book-loving community that my customers would love. We'd have a small membership fee, as the big bookstores did, but the difference between our program and theirs was that we had an escalating system that meant the more you spent in our shop, the more you saved. I knew my best customers would be thrilled to pay the annual fee because if they spent as much as usual, they'd save thirty percent on their books for most of the year. And even at a thirty-percent discount, I could still profit on the books. Not much, but more than my usual net profits when I included the revenue from the projected increase in sales and the membership fees.

When we were done, I put down the marker and plopped into a chair. "This is amazing. Thank you, guys." I wanted to hug them, but they were already beginning their self-assigned task of creating posters and social media posts. Walter had his tablet out and was sketching a design for a flyer.

"You're most welcome," Stephen said. "Now, go run your store. We've got this from here."

During the time I'd had this store, I'd learned two important things about my friends. One, they were the best around, and two, when they had a plan, it was best to get out of their way. So I kissed both of them on the cheek and walked back out onto the store floor.

Technically, my shift was done for the day, but Jared wasn't due for another half-hour. And I was pretty stoked about my shop after the planning session with the Arritt-Hitchcocks. So I decided to wander the floor, straighten the shelves, and chat with customers if anyone was inclined.

I had just made my way to the front shelves to arrange the new bookmark spinner I'd added to our merchandise when a woman with long silver hair, a flowing blue skirt, and the palest skin I'd ever seen breezed in and said, "May I speak with the owner?"

Her question wasn't directed in any particular direction, and given her ethereal quality, I wondered if she was speaking to unseen fairies or something. I didn't entirely discount the presence of fairies, mind you, but if they were in my shop, they had never made their presence known to me.

Fortunately, I was in earshot, so the fairies didn't have to hunt me down. "I'm the owner. Harvey Beckett. Nice to meet you." I put out my hand to shake hers, but instead of taking it, she took the edges of her skirt and curtsied. It had been a while since I'd seen a full-on curtsy, so I was a bit taken aback. "Malaysia Radison," she said when she stood back up. "It's a pleasure to meet you." Her face was soft and gentle, and when a small smile reached the corners of her mouth, I found myself smiling back.

"Well, you must be related to Car, and . . ." I almost said Mildred, but I didn't know if this woman knew about the murder. Honestly, I didn't want to be the one to break the news.

She smiled more broadly. "He's my big brother." The way she said it made my heart swell at least one size—if not three—because she said it with such affection.

"He's one of my favorites," I said. "What can I do for you?"

"Do you have a minute?" she asked more quietly. "I understand you were with Carson when he discovered our beloved sister."

I nodded. "I was. Let's go sit in the café. Have some tea?"

"Oh, I do hope you have coffee. I can stomach tea, but my stomach prefers dark, rich coffee." She smiled when she saw the cappuccino machine with Rocky beside it. "Americano, please," she said and pulled a tiny silver wallet out of a pocket hidden among the folds of her skirt.

Rocky smiled and made her drink along with my usual late afternoon vanilla steamer. Then we took our mugs to a table by the front window. "I'm so sorry about your sister," I said when we sat. "I didn't know her well, but it seems like the three of you were close."

Malaysia sipped her coffee. "We were. Mildred was always the strongest of the three." She looked up at me as she blew on her mug. "Everyone has always thought me a bit flighty," she said with a wink. "Wonder why?"

I laughed. Anyone who could poke fun at themselves got bonus points from me. "I'd love to hear more about her."

"My sister could have commanded an army if she had

wanted to do so, but she fashioned herself more utilitarian. More the tank in a brigade than the officer, I guess." She shook her head. "I'm not sure why I always turn to military analogies with Mildred. I'm a complete pacifist."

"She does sound strong. I know people like that." Mart was like that, in fact. She could organize anything, but she preferred to be in the midst of things, her hands dirty and her eyes sharp.

Malaysia sighed. "She had to be, which I realize now. I was always wandering through the woods and making sculptures from bark and such, so I wasn't around the house much when we were growing up, not if I could help it."

"Oh, that sounds both beautiful and hard," I said. I was fascinated by this idea of sculptures made from bark, but now wasn't the time to ask.

"That's childhood, isn't it? Beautiful and hard. I know now that our parents carried their own wounds, and while we never lacked anything we needed physically, emotionally our house was a pretty dark place. I needed more light." She paused. "We all did."

I swallowed and said, "I'm so sorry. That does sound hard."

She studied my face a moment. "If I may ask, how well do you know my brother?"

I smiled. "I'm just getting to know him. He's a lovely man." I wanted to be careful here because Car's story wasn't mine to share. "But it sounds like he had some hard years, too."

Malaysia sat back in her seat. "He's told you about his illness, then?"

I nodded. "He has. What a lot he has overcome."

"You can say that again," she said with a laugh. "Thank the saints for clocks. Those things saved him. Gave him somewhere to focus. He always said they slowed down his brain."

I didn't know what it was to have bipolar, but I did understand the idea of slowing my mind. Meditation did that for me. So did reading. "He handles them with such care," I said.

She looked away out the window. "For a long time, I think they were his only friends." She swallowed. "That's sad to say when you have two sisters, but I believe it was true."

"You were just children," I said as I put my hand on hers. "You were all surviving the best you could."

"We were just children," she said as she put a hand on mine. "And Mildred's way of surviving was control. She managed the house, even when she was a tiny girl. She kept it clean and tidy so as not to tax our mother. That way, Mother and Father could retreat into their work—they were mathematicians at the university—and at least be happy themselves, even if they couldn't do much to help us be happy."

A deep pang of sadness swept through me for all these kids and the tragic knowledge that Mildred carried the burden of caring for everyone. Everyone but herself, I imagined. "It sounds like Mildred didn't get much of a childhood."

Malaysia shook her head. "She didn't. Not a bit. She was the one who kept us all well, or at least well enough." She took a deep breath. "That's why it's such a shock that someone killed her. She was always so . . . so capable."

Normally, this moment would be the perfect chance for me to probe, to ask more questions. But my conversations with Jared and then with Stephen and Walter had cemented my resolve to let the police handle the investigation. "Have you talked to the police?"

"Oh yes, they were my first stop," she said. "That sheriff is so helpful and kind. I have no doubt that he will do all he can to find out who killed my sister." She paused and then looked at me. "I feel like I can trust you. Can I trust you?"

Inwardly, I sighed because I knew what was coming. But outwardly, I nodded. "Of course," I said, and I meant it.

"Something was going on with my sister. She'd been acting oddly for a few months now. It started when she followed Car here to St. Marin's," she said.

"I thought she followed him here because she thought she needed to look after him," I said before I could stop myself.

Malaysia nodded. "That's what Car thought, and me, too, for a long time. But then, when I'd come to visit, I'd see her squirreling around town like she was gathering nuts for winter. She'd buy butter at the farm stand but then go out to the dairy farm at the edge of town to buy milk before coming back into town to get flour from the grocery store."

I knew what Malaysia was getting at. Elle had all of those things from local sources at her farm stand here in town. "Maybe she wanted to buy direct?" Even as I said it, I knew that made no sense since the grocery store didn't stock local flour; they couldn't afford to.

"Again, that's what I thought, but it wasn't just things." Malaysia finished her coffee. "The last time I was here, she spent hours and hours at the library looking at old newspapers and printing random advertisements. When she'd come home in the evening, she'd place every page she'd printed into a plastic sheet and then into a set of binders."

That was odd, especially if they were just old ads. "Did she have some sort of project going? Some research on pricing or such?" I was stretching here, but I knew an economic historian who did just that kind of research. He was always gleeful when he found the prices of burlap in archival records—to each their own.

"Not that I know of." Malaysia looked at me for a long minute. "Honestly, I think she was trying to decipher some kind of code."

I sat back. "Why did you get that impression?"

"Good question. It was the way she kept comparing things to this one sheet of paper like it was a key or something." She shook her head. "Anyway, I told the police all about it, and they're going to look at the notebooks and such tomorrow."

I nodded. "That's good. If anyone can figure out what's

happening, it's Tuck and Jared." I meant what I said, and even though my curiosity was piqued, I still didn't feel the urge to offer help. "They'll definitely keep you posted."

Malaysia stood and smiled. "Thanks for talking to me, Harvey. I just wanted to thank you for being with my brother last night when he needed someone. You and your mother. He said you were both so kind."

I stood up and held out my arms. "May I?" When she nodded, I gave her a big hug. "Come by anytime you just want to chat or if you need another coffee."

"I will. Next time, I want to browse." She waved as she headed toward the front door.

I carried our mugs back to the counter, and Rocky said, "Did she say something about a code or something?"

I sighed. "Yeah, something like that. Seems a little too close to home with the notes that Marcus found, doesn't it?"

Rocky nodded. "This is all getting a little Da Vinci Code in here." She laughed. "Maybe you should invite Dan Brown to do a reading?"

"If it would get Dan Brown to come and do a reading here, I'd make up my own ancient mystery." I laughed and headed back to the store to grab my things.

We were definitely in the midst of, if not an epic mystery, at least a St. Marin's-sized one.

5

As usual, Jared was right on time—which, for him, meant five minutes early. I liked that about him because it meant I never had to worry if he was going to stand me up, a confidence I'd not had in all my relationships in the past.

Tonight, though, when he came in, he kissed me on the cheek and said, "I need to chat with Marcus for a minute. Do you mind?"

"Of course not," I said. "Bookstore stuff?"

He shook his head. "Murder stuff. You're welcome to listen in." He looked me in the eye. "But if you'd rather not learn more, maybe you'd prefer not to."

I sighed. It was a tough choice because, as it always was, my curiosity was ramming against my skull with questions. But my spirit, the deeper part of me, was quite happy to be out of this one. "I'll take the dogs for a walk and drop Sasquatch off. Meet you back here in fifteen."

"Perfect," he said and squeezed my hand.

The three dogs were raring to go when I hooked up their leashes. Fortunately for these three lazy mutts, "raring to go" meant ready to walk at a leisurely pace as they sniffed up what had happened on Main Street for the last few hours. We weaved our way down the sidewalk and greeted our neighbors, even stopping briefly by our friend Max's restaurant, Chez Cuisine, so he could give them a bit of pâté. Even though Max sourced it humanely, I never touched the stuff, but the dogs loved it.

By the time we got to the co-op up the block, the dogs had done the official meet and greet of the neighborhood, taken care of their bathroom business, and were ready to collapse and sleep again. The dog's life, I tell you.

Cate was working the front desk when we entered the co-op building, and I couldn't help but laugh. Her hair stuck almost straight out from her head, and she had a look of exasperation on her face that was almost comical.

"You okay?" I said.

"Oh, am I glad to see you. Could you hold this?" She stepped out from behind the counter and gave me a torso-sized balloon.

"Um, sure, but what is this?"

"It's part of our newest installation, a statement on the atmosphere by a local, talented artist." She sighed. "Most of the pieces are sturdier and wired, but this one is so hard to manage. I've been wrestling it all afternoon."

"I can tell," I said as I pressed the balloon between the counter and my body and smoothed down my friend's hair. "I have a couple of minutes. Can I help?"

Cate looked at me with gratitude. "Really? That would be awesome. Everyone else has gone home because of the snow and cold, and I need to have this hung for tomorrow's opening."

Had I realized my offer of help involved me standing on the welcome counter while Cate climbed a ten-foot ladder and leaned out to suspend the blue balloon from hot pink wire, I might not have offered. But still, we had the piece hung in a couple of minutes.

The walk back to the bookstore was only marginally faster without Sasquatch in tow, but when we walked in, Jared and Marcus were still deep in conversation by the travel books. I waved at Jared and held up my phone, a code for I'll text you.

He blew me a kiss and mouthed, "I'm sorry."

I smiled and headed back out the door with the dogs' leashes wrapped around my wrist so I could text Jared and tell him I'd get dinner started at his house.

With my text sent, I decided to take a longer route to Jared's. I'd already decided dinner would be simple—spaghetti, salad, and garlic bread, none of which would take long to make. Besides, the crisp air was invigorating, and the dogs and I could use more movement in our day.

I headed down the small walkway that we had landscaped between my building and the hardware store next door and admired the way Mom had used hardy herbs like sage and rosemary to fill the beds before planting deep burgundy pansies in front of them for color. The effect was holiday-ish without being gaudy, and I certainly liked these choices better than the ornamental cabbage that so many people chose for winter. I expected Elle had helped Mom out and steered her away from that far too common a selection and the rotting bodies of plants come warmer weather.

When I reached the alley behind the stores, I heard raised voices and cringed because the sounds came from the direction we needed to go. Still, I was already getting cold and didn't fancy a walk around the entire block to get to Jared's, so I tucked my head and urged the dogs to walk more quickly.

But as we got closer, I realized I recognized a couple of the shouting voices, and then I saw Car and Malaysia standing with a younger woman, all of them facing off in a small circle behind his shop.

"No, Indie," Malaysia said to the young woman. "We are not doing that. The police are handling it."

"Your mother is right," Car added. "Let them handle it."

"But she's my aunt, and someone killed her. I need to try to help," the younger woman, apparently Indie, shouted. "I can't just do nothing."

"You're not doing nothing. You can help us plan the service and work with me to decide what to do with her house. We have plenty to do without you trying to figure out what might have actually been nothing in some old newspapers." Malaysia sounded exasperated and tired.

"Don't you want to know what she was doing?" Indie asked, her voice now quieter.

I realized I had stopped behind a dumpster and was unintentionally eavesdropping, so I forced the dogs on and scuffed my feet purposefully to let the trio know I was nearby.

"Of course I do," Malaysia said. "But we're letting the police handle this," she finished as she turned toward me. "Oh, hi, Harvey. Out for a walk?"

"Just headed home for the night," I said. "Sorry to interrupt. Good to see you all." I smiled but then put my head down and picked up my pace.

I don't want to get involved. I don't want to get involved. I kept chanting this same mantra to myself.

Fortunately, none of the Radisons spoke to me again, and I felt, very noticeably, that I'd both stumbled into and avoided becoming mired in something I really wanted no part of. There was relief in that, and I decided that as soon as I got to Jared's, I would put the bread in the oven, boil the water, light a fire, and then mull some wine. We needed some holiday spirit tonight, for sure.

By the time Jared arrived home a half-hour later, the house smelled like cinnamon and cloves with a back note of garlic and tomato, the fire was crackling, and I was just pulling the pasta out of the water. "Perfect timing," I said as I plated his food. "You hungry?"

"How could I not be with my house smelling this good and a beautiful woman in my kitchen?" He walked over, pulled me close, and kissed me until I was slightly light-headed.

"Well, while I'm not ever going to be one of those women who loves to cook, that reaction to my cooking might warrant more of it on my part." I laughed and finished filling our plates. "Feel like eating by the fire?"

"It's like you read my mind," he said as he picked up our mugs of wine and led the way into the living room, where we set down the glasses and pulled out tray tables. We'd decided a month or so ago that eating by the fire would be a regular occurrence but that, in middle age, we needed tables for eating. Our laps were just not as flat as they'd used to be. Hence, the folding ones we kept stored behind the armchair now.

As we ate, I filled him in on the membership plan that Stephen, Walter, and I had created; he loved it.

"Could I suggest something, too? A membership event— maybe a special reading or something—once a year, just for members."

"Ooh, I love that idea," I said. "Rocky just suggested I get Dan Brown in. Maybe I should try for our first event."

"He'd definitely be a draw," he said. "Why did she suggest him?"

I shrugged. "Malaysia Radison came by today and told me about Mildred's weird newspaper obsession. I guess it sounded like a Dan Brown book to Rocky." I tried to sound casual, but really, I was dying to know what Jared thought.

"It actually does," Jared said. "We haven't seen the binders or the piece of paper she regularly consulted yet, but given the notes in the clocks . . ." He looked at me carefully. "I'll toe my line, but you keep an eye on yours. Stop me if I'm telling you too much for you to keep your resolution to enjoy the holidays?"

"I will," I said. "That's why you were talking to Marcus?" I shoved a far too large piece of lettuce into my mouth and wondered when my parents' extensive lessons on table manners would actually kick in.

"Yeah, he stopped by at lunch to talk to us about a couple of thoughts he had on the clues. He's good at that stuff," Jared said as he sat back with his wine. "Thanks for dinner. That was perfect."

"You're welcome. And I'm not surprised Marcus is a good puzzle master. Most readers are. It's part of the process, don't you think?"

Jared smiled. "Yep. I'm always trying to figure things out when I read, so that makes sense." He looked at the fire for a moment. "Actually, you know who might be helpful?"

"Galen!" we both said at the same moment.

"Exactly," Jared said. "Do you think he'd be willing to help?"

"Probably," I said. "Want his number?" I could feel my resolve fading a little at the idea of a puzzle-solving adventure, but for the moment, I could resist.

"Please. I'll give him a call in the morning." He put his arm around my shoulder. "If it won't be too much for you, could we meet in the store?"

"Of course," I said and felt a dangerous thrill of glee. "I can set you up in the group space, even put out a table."

Jared sat forward and then turned to look at me. "Harvey Beckett, I hear that tone in your voice. What are you thinking?"

I sighed and put my feet on his lap. "I'm thinking how much I love a good puzzle."

He rolled his eyes and downed the rest of his mulled wine. It was a fair reaction.

. . .

BY THE MORNING, I had convinced myself—well, deluded myself might have been a better term—into thinking I could work on the puzzle and not get too involved in the murder case itself. I knew myself better than this, but the idea of sitting by the fireplace with my friends as we worked on riddles outweighed my desire to keep the holidays light.

In fact, just before bed the night before, I'd asked Rocky if her mom felt like making gingerbread rolls for all of us, and Mrs. Chevalier had readily agreed. So I had, in fact, made our puzzle-solving extravaganza a holiday gathering.

Marcus was scheduled to open, but given that he and I would both be involved in the puzzling, I asked our friend Woody if he wouldn't mind coming in to help at the shop. Woody had been a professional woodworker for the last fifty years, making some of the best custom cabinets on the Eastern Shore. And in the summer months, when the warmer weather soothed his arthritis, he still did that work.

But he found he needed to slow down in winter, so a couple of months back, he asked if he could work part-time at the bookstore. "I know nothing about running a register, but I know the Shore and many of your customers."

"I can train you on the register, Woody," I'd said, "but what you bring far outweighs what you need to learn. How many hours a week?"

We'd agreed upon a flexible schedule that gave him about fifteen to twenty hours of work a week, enough for him to stay busy and connect to the community while also giving him time to work on some small projects as his arthritis allowed. He was now making a series of wooden nativities for Cate to sell in the co-op gift shop. They were beautiful, and I planned to buy one for myself.

With Woody set and happy to answer questions, consult Marcus and me when needed, and run the register, I got busy setting up our workstation while Marcus got the store ready to open. I put out a folding table and six chairs, expecting that both Jared and Tuck would come. Then I got a carafe of coffee from Rocky and set out the tray of still-warm gingerbread rolls that her mom had made for us.

We were ready to solve a puzzle and sell some books when the store opened. I imagined Rocky's second batch of gingerbread rolls scenting the café would also be a big seller. It was going to be a great day.

Two hours later, I felt quite differently. The table in front of us was strewn with notebooks and photocopies of the clues from the clocks, and all of us were stumped. Completely stumped. Galen had gone in first on the notebooks with what we had assumed was some sort of code sheet Mildred had created. He'd gotten nowhere. And then Marcus had run up against a brick wall, too.

Meanwhile, Jared and I had tried to make some sense of the clues from the clocks, but aside from knowing they were all time related and, thus, related to Car or at least his clocks—a fact which we knew, given where we found the clues—we hadn't gotten anywhere either.

And Tuck was working a more traditional police angle as he tried to put together timelines and suspects, and given his stern expression, it looked like he'd stalled out, too. We were a gloomy bunch.

Woody was holding down the fort well, and reinforcements —Stephen and Walter—had joined him to help drum up interest in the new book community—which we were apparently launching today. So far, their table with festive holiday décor and their jaunty Santa caps were drawing people in, and I could imagine they were selling a lot of memberships.

But I knew that if I got up from this table at this moment, I was going to break my mental momentum. While there was a place for letting my subconscious work on things while the front of my brain did something else, I could sense an insight at the tip of our fingers. "Are you up for giving it one more go, maybe as a group this time?" I said as a wisp of inspiration slid into my mind.

Galen, ever cheerful, immediately agreed, and Marcus nodded, too. Jared and Tuck didn't have much choice, given that this was their case, but they certainly didn't have to work it here with us. I looked expectantly at the sheriff.

"What are you thinking, woman?" Tuck asked, and I knew he was in.

"What if we just looked at everything as it is? Just read the articles Mildred pulled and set out the notes from the clocks as more of a message than a cipher?" I shrugged. "Maybe we're making this more complicated than it is."

Jared winked at me. "Says the queen of complicated theories herself."

"Hardy, har, har," I responded. "Want to give it a go?"

Slowly, everyone took a notebook, even Tuck, and I slid the notes from the clocks toward me before laying them in a column so they read like a poem.

He who mounts the stairs of time will find his demise.
The stitch in time never saves nine or ten.
Time's hands never move unless prodded with invisibility.
Abide with me, and I'll abide with time.
Time is never up . . . until it is.

I moved the pages around, changing their order, trying to see a pattern, a way the language became less cryptic.

Nothing got much clearer except that the "time is never up" line felt like the final one. Basically, the writer was saying that there was all the time in the world until time ends. *The apoca-*

lypse? Death? I marked the photocopy of that note with a five and pushed it aside.

From there, I just went with pure intuition. The idea of abiding felt invitational, so I put that one first. Then I moved on to the specific reference to time, nine or ten. Third, I placed the first note we'd found about the stairs, and then I only had the verse about time's hands.

Abide with me, and I'll abide with time.
The stitch in time never saves nine or ten.
He who mounts the stairs of time will find his demise.
Time's hands never move unless prodded with invisibility.
Time is never up . . . until it is.

The whole thing still felt foggy, but this seemed more right somehow. It also seemed less menacing. More personal, maybe. I called Marcus over. "What do you think?"

He studied my new order and nodded. "I can't quite say how that seems to work, but it does." He looked up at me. "The message feels sweet somehow now, doesn't it?"

I looked back at the papers. "It does." I had no idea what that sweetness meant, but it might come together somehow. "Any luck with the notebooks?" I asked the table at large as Marcus went back to his seat.

Everyone was looking quite intent, less frustrated now, and when no one answered except Marcus—"Nothing firm yet, but I'm working on a theory"—I took it that they might all have a lead.

I needed a latte and a stretch, so I patted Jared on the back and headed into the shop. On my way, I saw a woman sitting on the floor by the fiction section. She had a stack of books next to her, all titles by John Fowles. He wasn't an author I knew very well, but I'd recently started reading *The Collector* before I went to sleep and was hooked.

"Can I help?" I asked as I squatted down by the pile of books. "Trying to decide on which Fowles to read?"

She smiled up at me. "Oh no. I've read them all. Just on a budget and deciding which one to add to my collection."

"Ah, yes, the dilemma of ownership. I understand that. It helps if you have a bookstore." I laughed. "Well, if it's useful, I'll give you twenty percent off anything you choose."

"Thanks," she said as I stood up and reminded myself that squatting needed to be a thing of the past for my almost fifty-year-old body. I checked in on Woody, who said he was having a blast, and let him know about my special offer to this customer before getting caffeine. I desperately needed caffeine, and it was just shy of noon, so I could still have it and get to sleep at a reasonable hour.

As I had imagined, Rocky had sold out of her gingerbread rolls, and I was glad I'd gotten one over at our work table. "We still have a few left," I said as I pointed at the empty platter in the display case. "Want them?"

"Nah," she said. "Scarcity makes people come back for more."

I laughed. "Thinking like a true businesswoman." I took my latte. "Steady over here, though?"

She nodded. "Yep, going to be a good day." Then she looked at something over my shoulder. "Don't look. Really, Harvey, don't look."

"Don't look at what," I said as I leaned toward her. "Is Margaret Atwood in the shop?"

Rocky grinned. "You wish. No, there's just a man at the table by the window. Older black guy. Very stylish. He's been here all morning. Keeps buying things and putting back the magazines he's reading." She shook her head a little. "There's just something about him."

"An unusual bookish courtesy?" I joked. Most customers

never put things back, which I didn't really mind most of the time. "Want me to do my thing?"

Rocky, Marcus, and I had started a little game of "Guess the customer's story" a few months back on a slow day. Basically, we all formulated a theory about the guest—who they were, why they were in St. Marin's, and what they liked to read—and then, as the shop owner, I'd go over, introduce myself, and see what I could casually glean to see how right our theories had been. We only played the game with the customers who seemed the most interesting or lonely, and it always seemed to perk up someone's day when I told them, as I always did, that they had been the subject of our friendly fiction for a bit.

"I do," she said. "Here's my story. Widower. Loves carving model ducks. In St. Marin's on a bird-watching expedition. Actuary but has just retired."

"Ooh, actuary. That's a new one." I studied the man as I pretended to look out the window and sip my latte. "I agree on widower, but I think insurance executive. Here for a simple, quiet weekend away from Baltimore, his hometown. His favorite show is *The Sinner*."

"Oh my, that's very specific," Rocky said. "All right, Ms. Beckett, work your magic."

I smiled and headed the man's way. "Good morning," I said as I reached his table and extended my hand. "I'm Harvey Beckett, the owner of the shop. Just thought I'd say hi."

The man looked up at me and smiled. "Nice to meet you, Ms. Beckett. I'm Niall Baker. My pleasure."

"Do you mind if I sit a minute?" I said after shaking his hand. "I love having a chance to talk with customers."

His grin grew wider on his thin face, and I smelled the gentle scent of something lovely and floral, chamomile, maybe. "Please. I'd love that. I've been enjoying your shop all morning. You've created a beautiful place here."

"Well, thank you," I said and let the compliment sit in the air for a few moments. "Are you a reader?"

"Oh, yes," he said. "An avid one."

"Excellent. Any favorite authors or genres?" I found that any book lover loved to talk about the books they loved.

His cheeks reddened just a bit. "Well, it's a little odd for a widower in his seventies, but I do love steampunk."

I laughed. "That's incredible. Did you see our window display?"

"That's exactly why I came in. I love the clock theme, and I'm definitely going to pick up a few of the books you had there. *The Invisible Library* is one series I've been meaning to start," he said.

"Great choice and a big commitment. That series has gotten so long." I paused. "Or maybe you aren't like me and don't feel like you have to finish a series if you start it?"

He shook his head. "Oh no, I finish what I start. It's a habit ingrained, I'm afraid, by my career."

"Oh, what do you do?" I hadn't forgotten my conversation with Rocky, but I was thoroughly enjoying this chat with Mr. Baker.

"I'm retired now," he said. "But I was an actuary for fifty-two years. Can you believe it?"

One point for Rocky. "Wow, that seems like a hard career. So much science and numbers."

"You can see why I love to read, can't you? But I loved my work. I felt like I helped companies make good choices about their investments, and I learned a great deal about humanity in the process." He looked a bit wistful, and I wondered if he had missed it.

"Such important work," I said. "What brings you to our fair town?"

His face grew more somber as he stared out the window. "I

was hoping to see an old friend." He looked at me then. "You might know him. Carson Radison?"

A smile bloomed across my face, even as I pondered the oddity of two of Car's friends appearing this week in particular. "I do know Car. He's a lovely man." I almost mentioned that his clocks were part of our display, but I caught myself before I started talking about Mildred's murder with a man I had just met. "Have you stopped by his shop?"

"I did," he said, "but it was closed. Perhaps he's not feeling well?"

I sighed. "I can let him know you're in town if you'd like."

"Would you?" Niall said as his face grew happy again. "I'd be so grateful. Would you mind taking my number to pass along to him?"

"Of course," I said and typed it into my phone. "Well, I best get back to work, but before I go, I need to confess something." I pointed over toward Rocky. "The café owner, Rocky, and I had a bit of a chat about you before I introduced myself." I then explained our game and told him that Rocky had guessed his profession.

"Well, she deserves a gold star," he said with a grin. "Most people don't even know my profession is a profession."

I laughed. "Do you, by chance, carve model ducks?"

His head fell back as he laughed. "I do not. Was that her guess or yours?"

"Hers," I said. "Do you like the show *The Sinner?*"

"I'll give her another gold star for creativity, and if the TV show was your guess, you get a star, too." He waved to Rocky.

"It was nice meeting you, Mr. Baker, and I'll let Car know you're in town right away." I gave him a little wave as I walked back into the store. A lovely man, for sure.

6

Before I returned to my workstation with everyone else, I stopped by to see Walter and Stephen. The two of them were in their element, the extroverts that they were. No one got by them without at least a "Welcome to All Booked Up," and their charisma and welcoming faces had people stopping by without any suspicion or doubt, something that was rare when at a table selling something. My years of fundraising had taught me that most people are wary of being talked to out of the blue, and for a minute, I reveled in the fact that I had been a part of creating a place where people felt safe and comfortable.

"How's it going, guys?" I said as I grabbed a nearby armchair and dragged it next to Stephen. "Thanks for doing this."

"Oh, my goodness. It's so fun," Stephen said. "And we've sold about twelve memberships. People are very excited about the program, especially since it applies if they order books from you, too."

That had been a smart addition that Walter had suggested the day before so that the membership made sense for tourists and townspeople alike. "Awesome. And we did decide on free shipping for members, right?"

"Yep," Walter said. "You sure you can swing that financially?"

I nodded. "I have a budget line item for shipping, and we cover it easily. It shouldn't be a problem at all, even if this doesn't bring us more orders. But if it does, the book sales will cover any additional costs." It had taken me a while to get the hang of my books as a business owner, but now that I had, it felt so good to have a working knowledge of my store's financials. I was a lot less stressed than when we'd first opened.

"How about you guys? How's that going?" Walter tipped his head toward the reading space.

"Slowly," I said. "I think we're making progress, but we haven't had any major epiphanies yet." I sighed. "If you want to take a look, come on over. I don't think Tuck and Jared would mind."

Stephen nodded. "We'll go for another hour or two here until it slows down, then stop by." He looked out the door. "What do you think about a bookstore potluck tonight? Close up a little early and just relax."

"With your project," Walter said. "So sort of relax." He winked at me.

"I love that idea," I said. "Any main course you had in mind?"

"I have two crockpots of chili in our kitchen. Just ask everyone to bring their favorite fixings," Stephen said.

I shook my head. "You've been planning this all day."

Stephen sighed with a slanted smile. "Of course not. You know how I love freezer meals."

I was fairly sure the only thing these two had in their freezer was enough ice to furnish any cocktail glass in the state of Maryland. "Sure," I said. "Thanks." I dragged my chair back into place and hugged my friends. "Might invite Car and his family, too, if that's okay?"

"Good idea," Walter said. "They could probably use some company. The funeral is in a couple of days, right?"

"Yeah. The day after tomorrow. Tomorrow night is visitation," I said.

"We'll be at both," Stephen said before smiling and saying, "Welcome to All Booked Up. Might you be interested in hearing about our low-cost membership program?"

Gracious, he was good at that. I made my way back to the table to find my friends all talking excitedly and standing behind Galen's shoulder to look at the notebook in front of him.

"What's going on?" I interrupted.

"Look, Harvey." Galen pointed to a short article dated 1908 about a woman who had gone into the local general store and charged two hundred and eighty-seven dollars to her account. "She bought twelve bags of flour, four pairs of shoes, a fancy hat, and various other sundries."

The article went on to say that when her husband had come in and found the charge, he had been furious, especially since his wife was now in bed and not even using any of the things she had bought. She hadn't been out of bed for days, and the man had finally taken her on the ferry over to Baltimore to see a doctor. There, she was diagnosed with "manic depressive insanity" and committed to a hospital for treatment.

I studied the article for a long moment, and while I made a connection to Mildred and Car, I wasn't really in a place to share that information with everyone here. "So, what made that article stand out?" I asked.

Marcus picked up another notebook. "Here." He tapped another article about a young man who had run all the way down the Eastern Shore on a whim because he felt "like a god." When he was brought home to the town of Princess Anne, he hadn't slept in five days, and he wasn't making much sense. His parents had a doctor come in, and he was said to have manic depression. "All these pages talk about cases of bipolar disorder here in Maryland."

Jared flipped open two more notebooks, and on every page, there was an article about the illness.

"Mildred was researching bipolar disorder?" I said.

Tuck nodded. "It appears so. The question is why." He looked at me pointedly, and while I wanted to tell him and would tell him, I wasn't going to share Car's diagnosis with a whole group of people.

"That's a good question," I said. "Maybe you need to ask Car?"

Tuck nodded. "Good plan. I'll go see where he is right now." He picked up his ball cap and started for the door.

Before he got too far away, I called, "Chili potluck here at seven. Bring fixings."

"Sounds good. See you then," he said with a wave of his hat.

"Potluck, huh?" Jared said as he planted a kiss on the top of my head. "Perfect night for it."

"Closing early?" Marcus said as he surveyed the store. "Seems like a great idea. It's so cold out that it's already almost empty in here."

I followed his gaze and saw he was right. A few people were still browsing, and I knew we'd get a bit of a late afternoon run of guests, but it was already below freezing out, which meant the roads might be a little too iffy for most folks. We just weren't used to this kind of cold out here near the water. "My thoughts exactly."

I texted all our friends with the chili news as Jared gathered the notebooks and placed them back in the totes he'd brought them in. The responses were enthusiastic especially since most of us, with the exception of Elle, who had never been afraid of a patch of ice in her life, lived within walking distance.

And given that Tuck's response to the text was to say that Car was coming with his sister and niece—he'd beaten me to the invitation, obviously—I didn't think anyone would miss out, even if they had to drive in.

Sure enough, everyone responded with a hearty yes, and by the list of fixings that began to shoot through the air via our group text, we were going to have a feast. I was excited enough about the evening, given that friends and food were involved, but when Lu said she was making fresh churros, I was convinced it was going to be a spectacular evening.

Aside from taking Taco and Mayhem out for a late afternoon walk before the sun went down, I gladly spent the rest of the day at the store. With Marcus's help, we got the community program listed on our website, and I finished pulling the list of titles to return to the distributor. I even had a chance to talk about the merits of various Captain Underpants titles with an enthusiastic seven-year-old girl. It was a good day despite the fact that I was low-key mulling over Mildred's research the whole time.

I could understand her interest in the illness, especially if she had an inkling that her brother had it, and given that her notebooks were full of not just newspaper articles but also passages from well-known books and medical journals on bipolar disorder, she was diving deep. But it was the newspaper articles that were stumping me. What did she get from seeing how people with the illness had been treated? Even with my limited knowledge, I knew that people with mental illness, especially more serious ones like bipolar, had been traumatized by treatment and hospitalization. If someone I loved had the illness, I'm not sure I would have wanted to know all that history in detail.

By the time we closed for the night, I had mentally spun around to look at Mildred's research from all the angles I could imagine—a historical retrospective on the subject, a personal essay or memoir about loving someone who was bipolar, and a formal analysis of the history of mental health treatment. The options were pretty endless, but none of them really seemed to fit the nature of Mildred's exploration, given that she had both formal and journalistic sources. I just couldn't get it.

The wafting scent of spicy chili lifted the frustrated gloom I had let settle over me for the last hour, and when I saw that my friends had brought everything from cheese to chives to sour cream and crusty bread, I forced myself to let go of the query altogether and just relax. Rocky and I had contributed to the meal by buying out the rest of her pastry case for dessert, which was a win-win since she now had more cash and a fresh case for the next morning's delivery. No waste, no want, as Mom always said.

Mom and Dad brought, of course, a huge green salad for all of us because my father didn't think any meal was complete without something green, and to be honest, I probably had my relatively good health to thank for this belief that had been engrained into me since childhood.

By seven fifteen, we were all draped around the fiction section with bowls and plates of goodness.

"Do I smell cinnamon?" Bear asked as he sat down in the wingback chair beside me.

"Oh yes," I said with a wink at Lu. "Fresh churros, I understand. Rocky is just keeping them warm for us."

"Well, thank you, Luisa," Bear said with a circular flourish. "A perfect addition for the night." Bear, his wife Henri, and their best friend Pickle were always welcome. The men, especially, brought a grounded presence, maybe because they needed that quality for their job as a doctor in the ER and an attorney. Or maybe it was just that they were good ole boys of the best sort, St. Marin's natives who loved the place for what it was and what it was becoming.

"Bear, tell us about what St. Marin's was like when you were a kid?" I asked.

"Oh, yes, I'd love to hear about that," Car said from his chair across the makeshift circle. "I've been here only a few months, but I'm so intrigued by the long line of stories in this place."

Malaysia and Indie were sitting near him on the floor, and while they'd been polite enough when Car had introduced them to everyone, they had stayed pretty quiet.

"Well, when I was very little," Bear began in an accent one level richer than his usual, "the bridges weren't there. We had to take boats or ferries back and forth across the bay."

He continued regaling us with tales of the way the water really was life for everyone here, how his father was a fisherman and his mama could gut a fish in three seconds. He talked about running free around town and how each building had a purpose. "We had two funeral directors in town, and they fought for customers like nobody's business," he said with a laugh. "Not enough dying to go around."

The converse weight of Bear's words bore down on the room as we realized that, unfortunately, dying was all too common—and all too close just now—in St. Marin's. But I pushed past the ominous topic because Bear's stories had spliced together some of the ideas that had been swirling around in the back of my mind, and I had an idea that I needed to test.

I could see Bear getting ready to apologize to Car and his family for his poor choice of words, but before he could, I said, "That reminds me, which funeral home will you all be using to honor Mildred?"

It was a crass question, and I knew it. But to make more connections in these ideas, I had to know. Jared put his hand on my shoulder, a gentle reminder that I had promised not to intervene. I patted his fingers because I wasn't, not in the active investigation.

Malaysia looked at me and said, "Tompkins. It's always been our—" She stopped and cleared her throat. "We've heard they are the best."

Cate shot me a glance and then nodded. "Oh yes, they're quite wonderful. Respectful and dignified. They've been in the business for generations." She looked over at Bear. "Were they here when you were a kid?"

"Sure were," Bear said. "They've always been the best. Handled my daddy's services." He looked over at Car and Malaysia. "You made a good choice."

"That's good to hear," Malaysia said. She waited a moment, then said, "Can I ask you all a question?"

"Of course," Elle said from next to her. "How can we help?" We all leaned forward a bit, eager to show that Elle spoke for all of us in the most sincere way.

Malaysia looked out the window behind Jared and me and swallowed. "Would you all come to the funeral?"

Indie shot her mother a look of what seemed to be both confusion and frustration but didn't say anything.

"Of course, we will," I said as I glanced around at the heads nodding around the room. "We'd be honored. In fact, I think most of us were planning to be there anyway, right? And I already talked to Car about hosting a reception here after the service."

Again, everyone nodded. "How can we help you with things? Do you want one of us to pick you up?" Henri asked.

Tears threatened to spill from Malaysia's eyes, and when I looked over at Car, he was already crying. "Thank you so much," he said.

"Why would you do that?" Indie asked a little too loudly. "Why would you be so nice?"

Woody quietly laughed and said, "Why wouldn't we?" He smiled at the young woman. "We're a community here, Ms. A family of sorts, and we take care of one another."

Indie scowled, but she didn't say anything further. Still, she really didn't look happy.

Mom stood and said, "Okay, Harvey, where's that whiteboard of yours? We need to make a plan."

Marcus ran to the back room and rolled the whiteboard out, flipping it to the clean backside as Stephen, Walter, and Elle began cleaning up the dirty plates and filling the large trashcan I kept in the back room for events.

"I'll be your chauffeur for the next couple of days," Woody added. "Here's my number." He handed Car his business card. "Just let me know when and where, and I'll pick you up. No need for you all to be worried about getting around just now."

For a moment, I wondered just how Woody planned to transport three people and himself, but then I saw my dad slip Woody his car keys. They'd be riding in style for the next couple of days.

With hugs from Mom and me, Car and his family headed out for the night as the rest of us finished putting the store back in order for the morning. Marcus and I handled the register and business stuff while Mom helped Rocky in the café. The rest of our friends tidied the books and straightened chairs, as they always did after one of our potlucks. And within a half-hour, the store was spiffy and ready to open.

Mayhem and Taco had, as usual, managed to con some of my friends into giving them a dinner's worth of samples from our human food, and they would have been content to sleep off their food comas at the shop. I, however, was not content to clean up their bathroom messes when I returned, so Jared leashed them up and took them out while I locked up the store.

Being alone in this space at night was always a little special. So much had happened in this building over the decades it had stood, and we were layering new stories on top of the old. In the quiet of the night, I could almost feel those stories singing, and it was a beautiful, if not bittersweet, song.

. . .

THE NEXT MORNING, Marcus and I were both at the store to open. We'd planned the night before for him to take a long afternoon break before coming back to close while I went to the visitation for Mildred Radison. Tomorrow, we'd be open in the morning and then close for the midday service and the rest of the afternoon. The first thing we did when we got in was to make signs for the front door, the register, and the café with our hours for the next few days due to a "family emergency."

We'd just opened the door for the morning when Tuck came in and waved me over to the café. "Good morning," he said after he ordered his usual black coffee and my vanilla latte. "Have a minute to chat?"

"Of course," I said as I shot Rocky a look.

"You are both terrible at this," she said. "You do know that Harvey swore herself off investigating, right, Tuck?"

He rolled his eyes. "And you know that this woman is incapable of not trying to find answers even if she doesn't want to, aren't you, Rocky?"

She laughed. "Fair. Fair." She slid our drinks across the counter. "Off you go."

I sighed. They were both right. I honestly didn't want to be sleuthing, yet my brain didn't seem to be able to let things go. Curiosity was a mixed blessing.

After we sat down, Tuck went right for the heart of things. "Tell me what you were thinking last night. Why the funeral home question?"

If I was curious and asked a lot of questions, Tuck was astute and wise in a way that made me look like a little lost puppy. "I'm not sure it's anything," I said, trying to downplay my intuition, but Tuck just raised his eyebrows. "I'm wondering if the funeral home records might be a useful resource."

"How so?" Tuck said as he sipped his coffee. "Who would we be looking for information on?"

"That's the part I'm not sure about yet." I took a deep breath. "That thing Bear said about two funeral homes just sparked something in my brain. It might be nothing, but I keep thinking that Mildred was looking at those old articles about bipolar disorder for a reason."

Tuck nodded. "And you think she might have been looking at family history?"

I shook my head. "I really don't know. I just feel like there's something about the Radisons we don't know." A thought lit up my brain. "The past couple of days, two old friends of Car's have come to town." I went on to tell Tuck about Komiko and Niall and what I had learned about them. "They were both so nice, but it was just odd."

Tuck studied his notebook. "That does seem like quite a coincidence that old friends came the same week that Mildred died, doesn't it?" He ran his fingers over his shaved head. "What did Car say when you told him about Baker's visit?"

"Not much. He thanked me for the information and took Mr. Baker's number but nothing more."

"Nothing about how they knew each other?"

I shook my head. "Now that I think about it, his reaction was very, very quiet." My stomach clenched. "You don't think he might have killed Mildred?" That idea felt completely wrong to me, but I had been wrong about these things before.

"I'm just following the evidence, Harvey. Thanks for letting me know." He sighed. "I'll need Mr. Baker's number. You didn't happen to get one from Komiko, did you?"

I shook my head as I gripped my phone hard on top of the table. "I don't think Mr. Baker even knew Mildred was here or that she had been killed."

Tuck tilted his head. "Harvey, please. I really do need to speak with Mr. Baker and Komiko as soon as possible."

I sighed, opened my notes, and gave Tuck the number. "You will talk with Car first?" I don't know why it felt so urgent that Car be the one to tell Niall about his sister, but it did. "Please."

"If it seems that important, Harvey, of course. Explain what you're feeling to me, though." Tuck had long ago learned, as I had, that my sense of things was usually right, maybe not in a concrete sense but on some emotional level.

"I can't really put words around it, but I just think Car needs to tell Niall about Mildred." I paused. "And maybe it would help if you were there when he did." That last flash of insight felt sure and steady. "Yeah, I think that would be good."

Tuck stood. "I better get to it then. See you at the visitation tonight."

"Of course," I said. I walked back into the store and saw that Marcus was already at the register, so I walked back into the psychology section. I didn't know what exactly I was looking for, but I needed a moment to think.

As I straightened the shelves, I reminded myself that Mildred had been researching historical cases of bipolar disorder here in St. Marin's and the surrounding area. She had obviously been interested in the illness, which made sense since her brother had it. But why historical incidents? And why here?

My mind was blank on that account, so I shifted toward the funeral home idea. That had felt significant at the moment, yet I couldn't piece together why. It seemed important to look at those records, though, particularly from Tompkins.

A flash of insight whipped behind my eyes. Malaysia had started to say something about Tompkins last night but had cut herself off. I almost jogged to the counter and told Marcus I'd be back as soon as I could.

He shook his head and laughed, far too used to my whims of insight to ask any questions.

Tompkins Funeral Home was just up at the end of Main

Street in an old Victorian house that looked like it had been here for eons. The plaque on the front door, though, said 1890, so not eons, but still a long time.

I wasn't familiar with funeral home etiquette, so I spent a minute on the porch, wondering if I should ring a bell or something. But then I decided it was a place of business and gently opened the beautiful, wooden front door.

Inside, the house was gorgeous, with a wide entry hall with a staircase that led upstairs, a beautiful parlor to the left, and a library of sorts to the right. A gentle chime announced my entrance, and a white man who looked to be about forty with silvering dark hair came out to greet me.

"Welcome to Tompkins Funeral Home. I'm Leslie Tompkins. How can I help you?" He gestured to the library on my right, so I followed him into the room and sat in a wingback chair by the window as he took the one just to my left.

"My name is Harvey Beckett. I run the bookstore up the street. It's nice to meet you." I smiled.

"Oh, it is a pleasure to meet you, Ms. Beckett," he said. "I've been meaning to visit your store for some time. I apologize that I haven't made it down there yet."

"Well, I haven't been to your place of business before today either, so I think we're even." I winced ever so slightly, even though I'd simply been trying to be polite.

Mr. Tompkins laughed. "Fair enough, although I have to say that I'm genuinely grateful when people don't come into my place of business more often than is absolutely necessary." His face grew somber. "Which brings us to your visit? How may I help?"

I imagined it wasn't often that someone came in to see this man when they were lighthearted, and while I wasn't at my most joyful, given the visitation and funeral pending, I also wasn't in the throes of grief. So maybe my visit today would be a small gift for Mr. Tompkins. At least, I hoped so.

"Actually, I'm not in need of your services, although I hear wonderful things. I'm actually wondering if you might have historical records that are available to the public," I said, not sure exactly what tone to take—light and breezy because this wasn't about a current death or serious because it was about death, even so.

Mr. Tompkins sat back a little, and I could see him visibly relax. "Oh, we do have records. Obviously, for privacy, we don't make public the records for the last thirty-five years, but the others are readily available for researchers in one of our rooms upstairs."

As I studied this much more easy-going man next to me, I thought about a book I'd read a couple of years back, *Confessions of a Funeral Director,* and how the author had talked about the heaviness of his family's business. I imagined that discussing historical records might be a welcome reprieve for the people whose business was death day in and day out.

"Might I see them?" I said. "I'm not quite sure what I'm looking for, but I'm hoping I might help a friend." I figured it was better not to put him in the awkward position of knowing I was researching something related to one of his current clients. "If now isn't a good time, I'm happy to come back."

Mr. Tompkins stood. "Now is a lovely time. We're having a quiet morning. Let me show you where we keep the files."

I followed him up the gorgeous staircase to a room that had obviously once been a bedroom at the front of the house. A long, wooden table in the middle of the room was flanked by four filing cabinets, all clearly marked with letters of the alphabet.

"If you know the last name, you can search that way," he said. "But we also have an index by year if you need that." He tapped a binder on the top of one cabinet. "Please take your time, and let me know if you need anything. I'll be just downstairs in the office." He gestured toward the back of the house below me.

"Thank you so much," I said and pretended to study the filing cabinets as he left the room. As soon as he was out of sight, I opened the drawer that contained the Rs and skipped back until I found what I had hoped to see, a file marked Radison.

7

W hen I returned to the bookshop an hour later, I was a little dumbstruck by what I'd found. Apparently, the Radisons had been residents of St. Marin's for as long as Bear's family. At the very least, they'd come—or, more accurately, were brought—to St. Marin's for burial. I found records for Radisons from the early 1980s until the 1860s, when the files seemed to have begun.

A quick read of the Tompkins Funeral Services website confirmed that the business had been formed here in St. Marin's in 1862 because of the need to help bury the bodies of the young men who died in the Civil War. The family had buried both Confederates and Union men, and it appeared they had been one of the few funeral homes willing to bury the Black slaves who had died fighting with or for their white owners.

I studied the more specific notes in the Radison family file, including the death certificates copied there. Given the company's history, I wasn't surprised that the Tompkins had performed full services for the family members who had died from causes that seemed—at least to my uninformed eye—

linked to suicide. The mentions of hangings and gunshot wounds were frequent on the pages.

By the time I closed up the files and made the short walk back to my store, I was carrying a deep melancholy as well as a fairly solid conviction that the Radison family had a long history of bipolar disorder, a long, very sad history.

I was also certain that it was this tragic family history with the illness that Mildred had been researching. I still wasn't sure why, but at least I now understood why she was looking at historical newspapers. What a terrible thing to study about your own family. The information had certainly dampened my mood. I couldn't imagine what it had done to Mildred.

Fortunately for me, the bookstore was my happy place, so when I saw we were quite busy, despite the cold weather, my spirits lifted a bit. I suggested Marcus take off immediately and take Rocky with him since Maybelle was in for the rest of the day. They needed time together as a couple outside of my store. Plus, running the shop by myself would keep me busy, something that felt important after my discovery this morning.

As usual, an afternoon of recommending books was just what I needed. I convinced a teenage boy with blond hair combed forward in the way that seemed to be popular with a certain athletic set to give *House of Hollow* a try even though there was "a girl on the cover" because I thought, given what he said about his love of *Umbrella Academy,* he would really enjoy the novel.

Plus, a young mother had come in with her three gorgeous children and bought copies of all the Kwanzaa books for kids that we had in stock. "We're honoring our own stories more," she told me, and I wanted to hug her. After they were gone, I spent my free moments refilling the front window display and ordering a few more Kwanzaa titles for our children's section.

By the time Marcus came back at four thirty to relieve me so I could go to Mildred's visitation, I was back in the Christmas spirit, despite remembering halfway through the day to text Tuck and tell him what I'd found in the Tompkins's records. I didn't want to hide anything from him, but I also wanted to save him the work of going through the records himself.

His response had been short but kind. *Thanks, Harvey. I'll add this to our files. Also, I just spoke with Car and Niall. It was a good idea you had.*

Jared brought me a pair of black slacks to swap out for my jeans for the visitation, and once I changed and refreshed my makeup, the two of us headed up the street to the funeral home, where we found Mom and Dad, Tuck and Lu, and Henri and Bear waiting for us. We all made our way together to where Car, Malaysia, and Indie sat beside a beautiful cherry casket. The top was open, and inside, Mildred looked lovely. Her makeup was tasteful, and she was dressed in a lavender suit that was well-worn but in great condition. Clearly a favorite of hers.

After greeting the family, I stood a few moments by the coffin and silently said a few words to Mildred. I promised her I would help figure out what she was trying to discover in any way I could, even if I couldn't commit to finding out who killed her. I hadn't known this woman at all, but even still, at that moment, I felt like she affirmed my choices. Or maybe that was just my own wishful thinking.

My friends and I spent the rest of the evening in chairs on the other side of the visitation room, talking quietly while the townspeople came through to offer their sympathies to the Radisons. If there was one thing St. Marin's did well, it was to support people in the midst of their grief. I expected that Car and probably Malaysia and Indie, too, had already received casseroles and desserts to help ease the burden of life for the next few days.

I leaned over to Tuck. "Do you know where Malaysia and Indie are staying?" The question had come to me as I pondered what they were doing with all the food they were gifted. "They're not in a hotel, are they?" I couldn't imagine anything much worse than a hotel room at a time like this.

Tuck shook his head. "No, I suggested they move to the bed and breakfast at the south end of town. The owner has taken very good care of them."

I smiled. It was this kind of thoughtfulness that made me love my town more and more. "And she's taking care of the food gifts too?" I asked.

"Oh yes. She's been preparing what Car has received for all of them as lunch and dinners." Tuck reached over and squeezed my hand. "They're well cared for, Harvey. Don't worry."

I smiled at him and then at Lu, who said, "And your mom and I have everything set for the reception tomorrow. She even asked Mr. Tompkins to announce it at the end of the service so everyone could come."

"That's good." Sometimes, opening up my space seemed like such a small thing to offer, but given how safe and secure that little store made me feel, I could only hope it gave the same feeling to the Radisons.

The stream of visitors had been steady throughout the evening, and despite the fact that most everyone had been very courteous and not stayed long, I could see the weariness on the Radisons' faces as seven p.m. rolled around. "Henri, do you know if Max is open tonight?"

She nodded. "We were planning on going there for dinner after." She looked over at Car and his family. "I'll invite them to join us."

I sighed. I wasn't up for dinner out, but Bear and Henri were extroverts who would actually enjoy the chance to talk with the family. "Thanks," I said. I had thought Jared and I could take them, but now, I just wanted to go home, watch mindless TV, and let my brain work through what I'd learned that day.

Jared was working the night shift tonight, a usual part of his routine every few weeks. Tuck had been able to bring on a couple more deputies to cover more of the night details and also bolster the daytime police presence, but he and Jared both believed they shouldn't ask their colleagues to do anything they didn't do themselves. So each took a night shift on a Friday night once a month.

Normally, I was a little sad to miss a night with my fiancé, but tonight, I felt like maybe being home with Mart, the dogs, and Aslan was just what I needed. Symeon, Mart's fiancé, was away tonight, building another of his increasingly famous pizza ovens, this time for a celebrity whose name he couldn't share but had hinted might have been part of a certain club that no one talked about. I was sure Mart knew where he was and who he was working for, but I respected his business and the privacy of his clients and didn't ask, even though I was dying to know.

So it was going to be a girls' night in, complete with a new season of *Love Is Blind*, pad thai that Mart was picking up on her way home from the winery, and tangerine soda that we'd been saving for just such a night.

The dogs and I left Marcus to close up the shop, and the three of us took our walk briskly since the cold snap was still in place, and none of us, it seemed, wanted to linger out in it tonight. I did make them stop and wait outside for a brief moment while I ducked into the corner gas station and grabbed a Snickers for Mart and a Baby Ruth for me, but then we trotted the final few blocks and burst into the warm house with delight.

Mart was already there, and I was delighted to see Cate and Elle with her. "Your mom and Henri were invited," Mart said as she handed me my bottle of soda, "but both of them went out with Car and his family. So, it's just the four of us."

I was sad Henri and Mom were out, but I was also grateful they were taking care of the Radisons and that we were a small group tonight. It was hard to really sink into terrible television when too many people had opinions to share. My mom had more than her share of critical thoughts about reality TV, and she was not hesitant about sharing a single one of them.

Fortunately, the four of us were quite content to let ourselves be totally wrapped in the show, and by the end of the first episode, we all had our favorites for who would make it through the season and who would most definitely not. We'd watched enough of these shows to know that the people who started out bringing the most drama were probably the most likely to be healthy in a relationship since they knew what to do to stay on the show. Those who tried to be perfect usually hid some pretty big flaws, and when those came out, holy cow! Things got interesting.

After watching three episodes, we called it a night, promising to do it again soon, and Elle and Cate left to head home. Mart and I cuddled up on the couch and turned on *The School of Good And Evil*, a total teenybopper movie full of fairy tales and terrible wigs. It was exactly the kind of thing we loved.

The dogs curled up on their beds by the fire, and Aslan forced her way behind my legs and promptly started purring. Between the soft snores of the dogs, the rumble of the cat against my body, and the long day I'd had, I barely saw the two main characters reach the school before I fell asleep.

When I woke up with a crazy neckache and a thin line of Mart's drool on my cheek, it was morning. I unwrapped myself from my still-sleeping best friend and my awake but purposefully not-moving cat and went to the kitchen to make coffee. It was almost eight o'clock, and both Mart and I needed to get going for the day.

In these instances, the coffee grinder was a stellar tool for bringing the house to alertness. It was effective at waking everyone but was not typically resented because it promised coffee.

Mart stretched on the couch and said, "A full pot, please."

"Already on it," I said as I ground another batch of beans for our huge coffee pot. "You able to come to the funeral today?"

She walked over. "Yeah, the bosses were really understanding, so I'll meet you there a little before noon."

"Cool. How was your day yesterday?" I asked. By a silent exchange of looks last night, Mart and I had agreed to leave the conversations about work and such until today, when the light of the morning would help with perspective.

"Long but good. We got another distributor interested, so now I'm researching land so we can plant more to keep our estate designation." Mart had recently explained to me that the "estate" label on a bottle of wine meant that the vast majority of grapes had been grown on the property and then made into wine in the same location. Apparently, this designation made the wine more sought after, and the winery where Mart was now the vice president cared very much about keeping that designation.

"Well, look at you, Ms. Real Estate Tycoon," I said.

"Hardly," she said. "What about you? What's the latest?"

Mart and I always had a healthy string of texts going, so I had given her most of the updates about what had been going on. "I found something in the funeral home records."

"Wait, back up. What funeral home records?"

I recapped our potluck conversation in more detail than my text had allowed. "It got me thinking about whether or not the funeral home might give us more information."

Mart laughed. "So a random mention of a funeral home made you think that maybe the records of that funeral home—records I didn't even know they kept—might be a clue. Your mind is a fascinating place, Harvey Beckett."

"What can I say? I'm a random thinker." I shrugged. "So, do you want to hear what I found or not?"

"You have to ask?" Mart said as she poured us another mug of coffee each.

When I finished telling her about what I suspected about the Radisons' tragic history with bipolar disorder, she set down her mug and said, "Wow, how awful for all of them."

"I know. I can't imagine growing up and knowing there was a pretty good chance you could develop a serious mental illness. That must be terrifying." I'd had a pretty intense fear that I was going to have my father's feet—wide, hairy things— and I had worn closed-toe shoes for years because of it. No sandals for me. And wide, hairy feet were not a major mental illness, not even close.

"You told Tuck?" Mart asked after a few moments.

I nodded. "He's going to look into it and talk with Car about it, I think."

"Good. So you can just put that into his and your fiancé's capable hands and move on to more happy things, like Christmas." She smiled at me gently. "What do you have planned for the store this week?"

I welcomed the change in topic and gave Mart the rundown on activities that included a special *Polar Express* storytime with a model train in the café and a gingerbread house competition in the café later in the week. "It's going to be so fun."

As I got ready for work, I realized that I was looking forward to the week. The store was going to be full of holiday spirit, and I needed that infusion of joy for sure. As Mayhem, Taco, and I made the chilly walk to work, I decided we were going to up our holiday displays with a little live greenery if Elle had any left. I was in such a good mood that I thought I'd probably even enjoy sweeping up spruce needles every day.

The lights were on in the café but not the store when I arrived, and I smiled to realize that, for once, I had beaten Marcus to work. For a while now, I suspected that he watched for me to come down the street from his apartment near the other end of the road and then raced over just to show me up.

This morning, though, when he came in just after me, his usually playful expression was replaced by one of deep gloom. "What's wrong?" I said as soon as he returned from stowing his skateboard in the back room.

He shook his head. "I can't yet, okay?"

"Of course," I said. "Just know I'm here." I watched him walk toward the front of the store to tidy the window displays and frowned. He was deeply unhappy.

We went through the routines for opening, and when ten a.m. rolled around, a small group of folks was waiting outside, ready for books and coffee. I couldn't blame them, especially since we were closing in two hours.

When I went to the café for my morning latte, I found Rocky leaning against the door to her small kitchen. She looked absolutely exhausted and like she had been crying. Suddenly, I realized that what I saw in both of my friends was a romantic problem, a serious one, it seemed.

"Oh, Rocky," I said as I came around the counter to hug her. "Oh no. Are you okay?"

She shook her head. "No, not really. Marcus told you?"

I sighed. "No. He said he wasn't ready to talk. Do you want to talk?"

She nodded. "He proposed, Harvey."

Even though I had known their engagement was probably coming, I was still surprised to hear about it, maybe because I hadn't even suspected he'd pop the question now. "Okay, I thought that would be a good thing." I was very confused.

"Me, too, but when I went to say *yes*, the words *not yet* came out instead." Tears welled in her eyes. "I'm not ready to be married."

I pulled her to me in another hug. "It's okay that you're not. Really. Marriage is a big deal." She cried gently against my shoulder for a bit, and when she stilled, I said, "And how did Marcus take that?"

"Not well," she said as a bit of steel came into her jaw. "He assumed I meant no and stormed out of my place." She looked at me with grief. "I didn't mean no, Harvey."

"I hear you," I said. "You meant not yet. You said what you meant, but he could only hear his pain."

She nodded. "Men are so infuriating sometimes." I took it as a good sign that I could see flecks of anger behind the sorrow. Anger was actionable. Sorrow was debilitating.

"Often," I said. "Often they are." I grabbed her gaze and made her look at me. "You two will work this out. He will understand when he can get over himself."

She huffed out a laugh. "Any sense of a timeline on that?"

I glanced over where Marcus was stacking the shopping bags in a perfectly ordered pile. "I'd give him a bit," I said.

"Uh-oh," she said. "He's gone all super-Kondo. Better prep the back room." She smiled and then looked at me sincerely. "Thanks, Harvey. I feel a little better."

"Good," I said, "and if the opportunity comes for me to smack some sense into your boyfriend, I will snatch it up." I squeezed her arm and then made my own latte before going back to the book side of the building.

"Feel like straightening the back room?" I asked Marcus when I saw that he had moved on to cleaning the register keyboard with a cotton swab.

"You got it out here?" he asked.

"Of course. I'll call you if I need you," I said and watched him mope his way to the back. Maybe time alone would help him see a bit more clearly . . . or maybe I wasn't getting the whole story, and he had good reason to mope. He'd tell me when he was ready.

For now, though, a tiny girl with all the books from the Keeper of the Lost Cities series was waiting to pay for her books, and I couldn't wait to hear why she loved these titles. I hadn't read them yet, but maybe she'd convince me to move them up my TBR stack.

Marcus stayed in the back for the rest of the morning, and I hustled around to answer questions and run the register. By the time noon came, and I turned off the open sign, I was quite tired, and our back room was so organized that I thought the Holy Grail might have been discovered and shelved under H back there.

Mom and Lu came in just after we closed, and Stephen and Walter followed soon after. I left them to get things set up for the reception and went into the bathroom to change into my black dress for Mildred's service. When I returned, the tables were set up in the reading space with black tulle tastefully hung over the large window to give us a bit of privacy and to tone down the bright winter light a little.

When Dad, Tuck, and Jared arrived—Tuck and Jared in their dress uniforms and Dad in a beautiful dark-gray suit—we made our way over to the Methodist church a few blocks off Main. The building was beautiful, all brick with colorful stained-glass windows, and not for the first time, I thought that church buildings really were sanctuaries from the hardships of life.

Most of our friends were already seated when we arrived, and we slid quietly into the seats they had saved for us. I glanced around and spotted both Niall Baker and Komiko in the crowd. They must have seen the announcement in the paper, I figured.

A large painting of Mildred sat at the front of the room, and I immediately recognized the style. "You painted her portrait?" I leaned back to whisper to Cate.

"Car mentioned that they didn't have many photographs of each other, so I did all three of them." She gave me a small smile and then sat back.

Again, I was struck by just how kind and generous my friends were.

Just before one, Car, Malaysia, and Indie came in from a back room and took their seats in the second pew from the front. A woman in a long purple robe with a white and gold stole stepped onto the platform.

"Welcome, everyone," she said.

Her kind words about Mildred felt sincere, if a little distant, and I wondered if this was one of the harder parts of being a pastor—performing services for the people you barely knew.

Car and then Malaysia gave tender eulogies about how their sister had kept their household going, even in the midst of the chaos of their childhood. "That woman could use a broom to sweep and then to swat all in the same motion," Car said to a gentle chuckle from the audience.

After a final singing of "Amazing Grace," the pastor announced the reception at my store, and several of us ducked out to finish setting out the food Rocky had kept warm in her kitchen.

At the reception, the crowd was quiet and respectful. I appreciated that as Car, Malaysia, and Indie sat at a central table, many townspeople came and spent some time with them, especially since my friends and I were busy refilling platters and clearing empty plates.

At one point, Car assumed a stiff posture when Komiko joined him, and their conversation was brief and quite formal, it seemed. Komiko then waved and mouthed a thank you to me as she left.

As the gathering began to thin around three, we all sat down at or near the Radisons' table and quietly ate. It seemed like Car was small-talked out, and I couldn't blame him. If I was an introvert, Car was nearly a recluse in comparison. I imagined the day's events had been exhausting in all ways.

So I was surprised when he said, "Harvey, would it be possible for me to buy some books?"

I glanced over at Marcus, who nodded and said, "If it's okay with everyone, I'll just open the store. Then you can all browse, and we can invite in anyone who'd like to shop."

"I like that plan," Car said. "And perhaps we can share the rest of the scrumptious food?"

"You sure?" I asked. "We can pack it up for you to take home."

Malaysia put up a hand. "Please, no, we have so much food that we will need to eat nonstop for a week to get through it all." She stood and helped her daughter to her feet. "Indie, give me some book recommendations."

The three of them wandered into the shelves, and I turned the open sign back on. I was quite content to close the store for the day, but it did feel good to be open again, both for the revenue and because, somehow, it seemed good to give St. Marin's and our guests somewhere to be on this chilly December afternoon.

We had a surprisingly good sales day, and I was absolutely ecstatic to see that what Indie recommended her mother read was *Piranesi* by Susannah Clark, a brilliant novel about the place of truth and reality in a world of perspective.

"What did you love most?" I asked Indie as I rang up their purchase at our friends and family discount.

The young woman looked at me like I had just asked her if she preferred turtles to snakes and shook her head. "I don't know."

Her mother gave her a sharp look, and Indie said, "I liked that we didn't know who was telling the truth and who wasn't, but we still had a clear allegiance."

I smiled. "Same. It's interesting to think of truth as malleable by experience, huh?"

Indie stared at me, and then a small smile pulled up one

corner of her mouth. "Yeah, it is. It's interesting how we can think we know something with certainty even though it's completely opposite of what someone else knows."

"Exactly," I said as I handed her mom her bag. "If you have book recommendations, Indie, I'd love to have them. I usually am the one suggesting books. It would be nice to have someone else suggest them for a change."

"I'll think about it," Indie said with another smile. "Thanks." She and her mother walked out the front door as the bell chimed above them.

8

Many people who had attended Mildred's service stayed in the shop for the afternoon, browsing, sipping coffee, and just catching up with one another. Car also hung around, and I was so pleased to see that someone engaged him in conversation wherever he went in the store. From what I could hear, too, the chats had moved beyond expressions of sympathy into real discussions about his work and life in St. Marin's.

I was also glad Car felt comfortable enough to stay. I presumed his sister and niece had gone back to their bed and breakfast, and the idea of Car alone in that studio down the street was just too sad. Solitude was important sometimes, of course, but on the day you buried your sister, maybe it wasn't ideal.

As the gathering of customers began to thin around six, I looked over when the door chimed and saw Niall Baker. He was standing in the doorway, staring down the main aisle past the register to the fantasy shelves. I followed his gaze and saw he was looking at Car's back. Car was browsing the Sarah J. Maas series, and I realized he would probably love those with their fairy-tale-inspired themes and grandiose gestures.

At this moment, it was obvious that something very intense was about to happen. I didn't know if I, Car, or anyone else in the room could handle intense.

Fortunately, most older people have learned that powerful emotion doesn't have to accompany a spectacle, and Niall waited to speak until he was just behind him. "Car?" Niall's voice was soft.

Car froze for just a moment and then turned slowly. "Niall?" I studied Car's face, but I couldn't get a read on what he was feeling. Clearly, he hadn't seen Niall at the funeral earlier. There was no shock, but there was something—something deep. It didn't look like pleasure, but it didn't seem like disgust or any of its equivalents, either. "You came."

"Of course," Niall said. "I was at the service, too, but I didn't think it was the right time there." He reached out one arm and put his hand on Car's shoulder. "I was taking a walk and saw you in here. I hope it's okay."

Car's face settled into a soft smile. "It's very much okay." Then the men embraced, not in the way a lot of dudes did, with shoulders barely touching and lots of back-slapping. But in a full-bodied way, their entire frames lined up against one another. It was beautiful.

I realized it was more than just a friendship as the men softly kissed for just a moment before pulling apart and staring at one another.

"Holy cow. A reunion of long lost love?" Mart said at my shoulder as she joined me behind the register.

"It seems so," I said as I leaned against her and smiled. "Wow." As usual, my mind was swimming with nosy questions that I had no business asking, so when the two men walked by me, hand in hand, I simply caught Car's eye and winked.

He winked back. "See you tomorrow. Thank you for everything," he said.

"Absolutely. See you tomorrow." I watched the men wander out into the cold night, huddling closer together against the chill.

LATER THAT NIGHT, as Jared and I snuggled together by his fireplace, I told him about the bookstore reunion between Car and Niall. "It was one of the most beautiful things I've ever seen," I said.

"Wow," he said as he snuggled next to me. "That'll be us, you know?"

I sat back and forced a frown onto my face. "What, you're going to break up with me so we can have an epic moment when we're in our 80s?"

He shook his head. "No, drama queen. We're just going to have those epic moments for the next fifty years." He kissed me softly, and then we stared into the fire some more.

Something was poking at the back of my mind, and I couldn't quite grasp it. I kept thinking about *Piranesi*, about how it had reminded me both in concept and world of that Escher drawing with the stairwells that twisted and turned in ways that were actually impossible but also not.

"Question," I said as I looked at my fiancé. "What do you do when you have two eye witnesses for the same event but who see completely different things?"

Jared put his head against mine and said, "Oh, so every time we have two eye witnesses, you mean?"

"Really?" I said, sitting up. "It's that frequent?"

"Mostly. Sometimes it's just simply a matter of the angle from which someone sees something. They might think someone is quite tall or quite short. But sometimes, it really is about the witness's internal perspective."

"For example?"

"Well, once, a woman reported a violent dispute between her neighbors. Called in to say they'd had a serious break-up, and now she was throwing all his things out their apartment window and trying to hit him with them." Jared grinned.

"And the other witness?"

"In this case, it was the couple themselves. It turns out they were just moving and didn't want to carry everything down the stairs. They'd argued about who would carry what and then had decided to simply eliminate the question altogether and use the window." He laughed. "It was pretty ingenious, really."

"That is smart," I said. "I take it she didn't hurl a TV or something."

He shook his head. "Just soft stuff."

I settled back against Jared's arm. "So, what you're saying is that the idea someone brings to something informs how they see it, even in police cases?"

"Yep."

I nodded. I could see that. Twenty-five years ago, sitting on a couch and watching a fire would have seemed like a totally lame thing for me to do. I would have felt like a social failure to have chosen a night in if I could go out. Now, though, this was just about the perfect kind of night—a man I loved, a comfortable place to be, and a fire to warm the room.

"What's got you thinking about this?" he asked.

I told him about the book Indie had recommended to her mom and how it played with this idea of perception and reality. As I described the book, I felt a prick of something at the back of my brain again. "I think I might need to talk to Indie about Mildred," I finally said, and as I did, something confirmed that notion right in the center of my chest.

"Really?" Jared said as he squeezed me a little tighter. "Because her aunt was murdered or because of the idea of perception?"

I sat forward again and looked at him. "Honestly, I'm not sure. I really am not interested in trying to solve Mildred's murder, but something is prodding me, pushing me to figure out what question I need to answer."

Jared looked at me. "Then you need to ask." He kissed my forehead. "Living the questions only goes so far."

"Did you just quote Rilke to me?" I laughed.

"What? No, not me," he said with wide eyes and a smirk.

A few moments later, I said, "I love you."

"I love you, too," he whispered.

9

The following morning, the dogs and I made our trek from Jared's to the store by way of Indie and Malaysia's bed and breakfast. Nothing in St. Marin's was far from anything else, and while I didn't want to disturb anyone, I did think it a good idea to leave a note for the women first thing. I figured a note would convey a more serious interest than a simple phone message.

Besides, the temperature was warmer, and it had been a couple of days since the dogs had gotten in a good walk. Even their lazy selves had seemed a bit antsy this morning, so I figured they could use the chance to burn off some energy.

The Woodlawn Bed and Breakfast was in another of St. Marin's gorgeous Victorians, painted with all the colors of the most extravagant examples of architecture, with a soft pink trim against a darker pink background. It wasn't to my taste, but it was beautiful.

Given that it was after eight, I figured the owner would probably be up, so I let myself into the lobby and waited for the rustling I heard in the back of the house to move forward. A small, older woman who looked a great deal like Mrs. Claus came from the back and wiped her hands on her reindeer-clad apron before shaking my hand. "How may I help you?" she asked.

"I'm just hoping to leave a note"—I held up the small envelope in my hand—"for one of your guests, Indie Radison. If it's not too much trouble," I said.

The woman's entire face folded a bit when she smiled. "Why don't you give it to her yourself, my dear? She's in the dining room. An early riser, that one." She pointed toward a set of gorgeous pocket doors and said, "Just through there. Would you like some coffee?"

"Oh goodness, if it's not too much trouble," I said. "Thank you."

"No trouble at all," Mrs. Claus said and slipped back through a swinging door that I presumed led to a kitchen.

I slid the doors to the dining room open and saw Indie sitting, a book in front of her, at one side of the long dining tables. "May I join you?" I said as I waited by the door.

"Oh, hi," Indie said and slowly closed her book. "Sure." She looked at me carefully. "Are you staying here?"

"Oh no. I just came by to drop off a note for you, actually. Your hostess told me you were in here."

Just then, another door at the back of the dining room opened, and Mrs. Claus came in with a carafe and a "Marylanders Get Crabby" mug that she set beside me.

"Cream and sugar are on the table," she said and then slipped into the back again.

"A note for me." Indie looked at the envelope I'd set beside my mug. "What does it say?"

I poured my coffee and filled it with cream and sugar before answering. "It's sort of a strange question, I know, but I wondered if you had any theories about what happened to your Aunt Mildred."

All night, I had tossed around the fragments of ideas

floating in my head. Finally, around four a.m., after I'd captured a couple of hours of sleep, the question came to me from a dream where I'd been in the alley behind my store and seen Indie there with a magnifying glass. She was studying the wall because someone had glued newspaper articles all over it.

When I'd come fully awake, I knew what my brain had been trying to tell me, and I also knew I needed to caution her about how dangerous getting involved in a murder investigation could be.

She studied my face for a moment and said, "She was going to expose something that other people didn't want to be known." She didn't hedge her words or inflect them like a question. She was absolutely certain.

"How can you know for sure?" I asked as I lifted my coffee mug to my lips. The coffee was amazing, but I also didn't want to appear too interested in what Indie said. I figured she was still young enough to be skeptical of too much interest from an older adult.

I read that situation wrong, though, because the young woman fully turned her chair to me and said, "You really want to hear what I think?"

I put my coffee mug down and turned my chair to face her, too. "I do."

The first full smile I'd seen on her face lit up her features, and she said, "Great. So my aunt researched the history of bipolar disorder here in St. Marin's." She looked at me. "But I expect you already figured that out."

I nodded, not wanting to discourage her or give away elements of a police investigation.

"Okay, so I've been trying to figure out why. Why was she investigating that topic, and why might someone kill her for it?" Indie tapped her finger rapidly on the table, her nervous enthusiasm too much to be contained in words.

"I had the same questions," I said mildly. "Do you have any theories?"

Again, she grinned. "Well, I think someone in my family, maybe several *someones*, had or has bipolar disorder."

My stomach sank. She didn't know about her uncle's illness, and I certainly wasn't going to be the one to tell her, not if her mother and uncle hadn't. "I thought the same thing might be possible. What led you to that conclusion?"

"Well, I'm not absolutely certain because none of the people in the articles that Aunt Mildred found were Radisons. But she had this journal." She pulled a slim blue book out from under the one she'd been reading. "And here, she says she's trying to find—" Indie interrupted herself and opened the journal. "She said, 'I'm almost certain it's not me, but it does seem that someone in every generation has this curse of cyclical madness.'"

I studied Indie's face and then looked down at the book. "She thought she might have bipolar disorder?" I felt a massive sadness settle on my chest.

"For a while, but then she saw a psychologist and was diagnosed with depression. Still terrible but not as wild an experience as bipolar," Indie said quietly.

I nodded. While no diagnosis of a mental illness was easy, and depression could certainly be deadly for some people, I had to agree that, from my perspective at least, bipolar did seem absolutely wild and brutal. I forced myself back to the question of Mildred's research. "But am I understanding correctly? She thought at least one person in every Radison generation had bipolar disorder?"

Indie nodded enthusiastically. "She did, and since the illness is usually genetic, she was probably right." She stared at her aunt's journal. "But I can't prove that. I haven't been able to find any notes of any of our family members in any hospital records."

I let a long slow breath out through my closed lips as I tried to decide on the right thing to do. My brain said I should let Jared and Tuck know about the journal and suggest they talk to Indie. But my spirit, the part of me I was learning to trust more and more, said the right thing was to tell this young woman about what I'd found.

I went with my heart. "Indie, your aunt was right, and you can find the proof you're looking for in the Tompkins Funeral Home records. I looked at them a couple of days ago." I moved my chair closer to hers. "They've got the death certificates for most of your family, and while there's nothing specifically about bipolar disorder in them, the causes of death . . ."

Indie's face grew stone still for a few moments. "Are you serious?" she said in almost a whisper. "Okay. Well, thanks," she said. "I'll go look at them later today."

"Are you okay?" I said, a bit baffled by her reaction since I'd just confirmed her theory and given her more information about her aunt.

She shook her head slightly and then smiled in a way that reminded me of the school picture day smile. "Of course. Thanks for the information, Harvey. I appreciate it."

"Um, okay," I said and finished my coffee. "Well, glad I could help, I guess," I said as I stood to go. "You're sure you're okay?"

"Totally," she said as she opened the book that had been sitting on the table beside her, a copy of *We Are All the Same in the Dark*. "See you later." She didn't even look up as she spoke.

Outside, I untied the dogs' leashes from the tree in the side yard and let them lead me to work. I had clearly said something that upset Indie, but I didn't understand what. She had been very invested in finding out what her aunt was researching. Maybe I had ruined the fun of the hunt for her by giving her the information about the records. If that was the case, I did feel bad. I hated any kind of spoilers, even for things I wasn't that invested in.

Still, her response bothered me, but since I had no idea what to do with my discomfort, I decided to shake it off and go about my day. If there was a way I could make right what I had unknowingly done wrong, I'd find out at some point and take action. Until then, I had a store to prepare for a big holiday bazaar.

WHEN I ARRIVED at the shop, Marcus was already there, and from the sheen all the bookshelves had, I gathered he had been cleaning, which meant he was still pretty upset. And since Maybelle was in the café instead of Rocky, I took it that things had not improved for either of them overnight. I couldn't handle it.

"Marcus, let's talk," I said, realizing I was completely scrubbing out any line between co-worker and friend with this demand and not caring. We'd already erased that line, and with all that was going on, none of us could really tolerate the cloud of sadness coming off my assistant manager.

He looked at me and nodded. No resistance, which I took as a good sign. "Maybelle, can we get a vanilla latte and a double espresso, please?" I said as we walked into the café.

"Sure thing," she said with a soft smile. Clearly, she knew something was up, too.

When we had our mugs, we headed back to the fiction section, and I said, "She didn't say no, Marcus." I figured there was no value in pretense here.

"I know," he said, "but now I've screwed it all up so bad that I don't think we can come back."

I laughed, then quickly apologized before saying, "You love her, right?"

"Of course, I love her," he said with a spark of anger in his words.

"And I know she loves you, so there's nothing you can't put right if you want to do that." I truly believed that, and I knew that when he wasn't in a sorrowful state, Marcus was just as much a romantic as I was. "You need to tell her."

He sighed. "Yeah." But then he shook his head. "I just don't understand why she couldn't say yes, though. Then we could have decided to have a long engagement."

"You'll have to ask her that, but if I had to guess, she's overwhelmed by running a business and going to school. Maybe it's just too much to think about shifting her life right now." I could not possibly handle all that Rocky did on a daily basis. Maybe she was at her limit.

Marcus looked at me with his dark brown eyes and let out a long breath. "I should have thought of that." He scrubbed a hand over his chin. "It's just that things are going so well. Her business. My book. Things here at the store . . . I got excited and wanted to share all this with her."

I understood, probably more than Marcus knew. I was the kind of person who added on more good things when things were good, but fortunately, I had learned that even too much of a good thing was just too much. He would come to understand that in time, maybe already was beginning to understand now. "I think if you tell her that, she'll get it. But then you need to listen, too. Really hear what she's saying, not just how it makes you feel."

He stood up. "Okay. Can I get a couple of hours off?"

"Of course," I said. "Take the day if you want. I've got things covered here, and Woody is coming in later anyway."

Marcus was all arms and legs, so when he hugged you, it was a bit like being wrapped up in a tall tree. "Thanks, Harvey," he said. Then he walked out the front door, flipping the open sign on as he went. Ten sharp, no matter what.

. . .

THE MORNING SPED ALONG NICELY, especially when Mom, Stephen, and Walter descended with Car to begin plans for our Mental Health Association fundraiser in conjunction with the bazaar next weekend. Mom had asked if we'd set up a table for her and Car, and I'd agreed readily. I loved helping our community, and this was a win-win for both of us.

"So, I thought we'd put our table here," Mom said to Car as she waved to me and moved around like she owned the place. "Then we can have our banner, an array of informational brochures, and the credit card system to take donations. How does that sound to you?"

Car smiled. "That all sounds lovely, and thank you." He glanced over at me. "Niall and I will be here all day to staff the table. Thanks for putting us in touch."

I gave him a thumbs-up since I couldn't speak from being a little overwrought with emotion to see him smiling during such a hard time. Then I turned to where Stephen and Walter had, again, set up their membership table. "Gentlemen, I may have to start paying you."

Walter waved a hand. "No way. This is fun. I actually like selling things, and I don't have to manage a single project while I'm here. Well, except for Stephen," he said with a laugh.

"Ha," Stephen said. "Seriously, Harvey, this season is slow for both of us, and it's fun to be out in all the holiday hustle and bustle."

"Okay, then," I said. "Coffee?"

Both of them nodded enthusiastically, so I went to get our orders from Maybelle, who was holding down the fort very well in the café. She had a full house, and there wasn't even a line at the register. "Let me know if you need me," I said as I took our mugs.

"Will do, Harvey," she said as she turned her gaze to the man behind me in line.

Since my few customers were browsing without need of me, I decided to set up at the register and get the plans for our part of the bazaar ready. The events were already nailed down since they'd had to go into our newsletter last month, but I still wanted to offer a couple of special events. I decided we'd have some mystery book sales like the ones I'd seen online. We'd wrap books up in holiday paper and charge the same price for each of them. That way, shoppers could buy a couple and be rewarded with the chance to open a present and find a new book.

We'd need two categories—adults and children—and I wanted to be sure the books were worth at least as much as everyone paid. So I decided on a twelve-dollar price point. That way, everyone would get a great book for a low price, and I'd still make a little profit if I chose the titles wisely.

I was halfway through choosing the twenty-five classic novels and picture books I'd decided to feature when Komiko came in. When she saw me in the fiction section, she waved before heading back toward the history shelves. Her trajectory reminded me that not everyone was an avid reader of fiction like I was, and I decided to add a couple of popular history and business books to my collection.

When I reached for a copy of *A Little Devil in America*, Komiko startled me by stepping out from around the corner and saying a cheerful, "Hiya."

I dropped the book I was so surprised but then recovered with a cheesy, "Hiya back, Komiko." I put Abdurraqib's book into my basket and said, "You stayed after the funeral?"

"I did," she said. "I don't have to be at work today, so I grabbed a room at that great bed and breakfast and treated myself to a day away."

I wondered if she stayed at the Woodlawn like Malaysia and

Indie but decided that was too far out of my business for even me to ask. "Nice. Can I help you find anything?"

"This any good?" she asked as she held up a copy of Iris Chang's *The Chinese in America.*

"I've heard great things but haven't read it myself. I think my assistant manager has, though. He should be back soon if you want to hang out and ask." For some reason, it felt like a good idea to keep Komiko around, but I couldn't put my finger on why yet.

I texted Marcus and asked him to come back in if possible and explained why. He responded almost immediately to say he'd be in soon.

"Oh, cool. I want to pick up a couple of novels, too, so I'll browse. Maybe you can send him to find me when he gets back?" she asked as she tucked the book under her arm.

"Absolutely," I said and continued on my book hunt. It wasn't unusual for people to find our town and decide to stay for a bit. It was a quaint, charming place, after all. But something about Komiko's lingering presence wasn't sitting right with me. I reminded myself, though, that her choices were none of my business and went to the business section to grab a copy of *You Are a Badass at Making Money.*

With my selection of titles complete, I headed to the register to drop them off. I then gathered the wrapping materials I needed for this venture and for the wrapping station that I spontaneously decided to add as a gift to our customers.

Just as I was about to make a mad sprint into the back for the table, Marcus and Rocky walked in the front door. Given that they were smiling and holding hands, I assumed they had patched things up. And my impression was confirmed when Rocky came over to show me a gorgeous topaz stone set in a copper setting. It was a one-of-a-kind ring and perfect for my friend.

"You said yes?" I asked.

"I did," she said. "I explained that I couldn't plan a wedding right now, but I did want to marry him. He listened and then put this on my finger. I can't believe it."

"Yahoo!" I shouted loud enough to startle several customers, and then I looked at Rocky for permission.

"Feel free," she said with a blush.

"Rocky and Marcus just got engaged," I shouted into the store. "It's a great day!"

Everyone erupted into applause, and even though Marcus had gone back to work restocking our holiday window display, he and his fiancée were surrounded by well-wishers for several minutes. It was a true celebration, one we'd have to formalize with a potluck with friends soon. For now, though, I wanted to let them bask.

Fortunately, since my staff was very appropriately distracted, Woody came in for his shift. With his help, I got the wrapping station set up and decorated near the register, and then we wrapped up all the books for the mystery sale next weekend. I decided to do a big gift basket of holiday books and trinkets from our gift section to raffle off as a door prize next weekend, with all the proceeds going to the Mental Health Association.

When the well-wishers gave him some space, I told Marcus that Komiko was looking for his advice on a book, and he went off to find her while Rocky went to assist Maybelle with the steady stream of lunch folks coming into the café. Between their guests and the book shoppers, this was looking to be a banner day for the shop.

Even Mom and Car were getting a lot of donations, and when I stopped by the table, Stephen and Walter said they had already sold a dozen memberships. Sometimes we had days like this, where everything just flowed without me having to press or strive. I wondered if this was maybe the way life was supposed to feel, easy and successful without strain. I hoped so.

Alas, the easy mood didn't last long because a few minutes later, Marcus came back to the register with a strange expression on his face. "So Komiko wanted book recommendations, right?"

"Right," I said with my eyebrows up near my hairline in curiosity. "Did she not ask you about the Chang book?"

"Oh, no, she did, but she also asked me about Car. She said she was a little afraid to come back up to the front of the store because he was sitting there." He shrugged.

I looked at him and then remembered Komiko had not spoken to Car when she came in. I hadn't thought anything of it at the time because he and Mom were still setting up, and since their table wasn't right in front of the door, it was easy enough to miss them. But now, that did seem a little odd. "Did she say why?"

"No. I asked her if she was okay—if she needed help." He shook his head. "She wouldn't tell me anything but said she'd be ready in a couple of minutes and wondered if I'd walk her out after she bought her books."

Car was sitting and smiling at Mom, the picture of placidity and calm. I couldn't imagine for a moment that he would be dangerous to anyone, but I did know that looks could be quite deceiving sometimes. "Alrighty then," I said. "We are now providing escort services."

Marcus quirked an eyebrow. "You might want to rephrase that, boss?"

I laughed. "Oh, I don't know. It might be pretty lucrative," I said with a wink. "Thanks for helping her out," I said.

"Of course," he said as he headed back toward the fiction section to find Komiko.

A moment later, they returned to the register, and I rang up her three books before Marcus walked with her toward the door.

"Hi, Komiko," Car said as they walked by his table. "I didn't know you were in here. Find anything good?"

Komiko blushed a deep, dark red. "Just some light reading. See you later." She scuttled out the door, leaving both Car and Mom a little surprised.

"Did I say something?" Car asked Marcus as I walked over.

Marcus shrugged. "She wanted me to walk her out of the store because she said she was afraid of you." The look on Marcus's face was apologetic.

"That's weird, right?" I said to Car. "Any idea why she'd be scared of you?"

Car looked stricken. "None at all. Oh, that's horrible. Maybe I should go and talk to her?"

Mom put a hand on his arm. "I don't think that's the best idea, although I understand the desire to clear the air. If she's scared, then she's not in the best frame of mind to talk."

Car took a deep breath. "Right. That makes sense. Maybe she's having a bad day."

I remembered what Komiko had told me about her depression. I knew that sometimes anxiety was one of the symptoms of depression that cropped up for me. Maybe that was true of her, too, although this seemed a little more serious than anxiety, as debilitating as that could be. "If I see her later, Car, I'll try to figure out what's going on, for her sake and yours."

"Thanks, Harvey," he said. He nodded, but I knew this would weigh on him. It would certainly weigh on me.

THE REST of the afternoon was a blur of book sales, customer requests, phone calls about the holiday bazaar, and well-wishing friends coming to congratulate Marcus and Rocky. By the time I left at six, an hour later than planned, I was plum tuckered and glad that Jared and I had made plans to go out to dinner and a movie. Sometimes, it was nice to stay in—most of the time, actually—but it was also nice to go someplace where they washed the dishes, and the film was in surround sound.

We were going to see some Irish film that Jared had said got rave reviews. Honestly, I'd see almost anything in the theater. I just loved the experience. He'd chosen a theater that served dinner while we watched the movie, and I settled in with a great burger, some well-done fries, and a caffeine-free Coke—a rare luxury for sure—and loved the film.

On the way home, we decided to stop by Max's restaurant for dessert because I was craving this French rice pudding he'd just added to the menu. Jared didn't particularly love Max because Max was a bit of a prig sometimes and because Max and I had, very briefly, dated, but he was willing to put aside his preferences for a delicious dessert . . . and for me, of course.

Main Street was quiet when we parked by Chez Cuisine, and I could see that Marcus was busy tidying the store in antici-pation of closing up soon. A few tourists wandered the streets, but by and large, the street was empty.

Maybe that was why I noticed the shape of someone moving quickly along in the shadows on the other side of the street. Something about the way they were moving made me think they didn't want to be seen, and when Jared asked me to wait by the car for him, I knew he'd seen and thought the same thing. Something was going on.

"I'll go into the store," I said because I needed to pick up Taco and Mayhem anyway. And if something was going to go down, I knew Jared would rather not have to think about me.

"Good plan," he said as he kissed my cheek. "Let Tuck know?"

"Of course," I said as he started to whistle and walk up the street in what, I assumed, was a plan to double back on the person.

I sent my text to Tuck before I was even inside, and when I told Marcus and Rocky what was happening, we all stood, lights out in the café, watching from the window. Jared moved quite quickly despite his casual demeanor, and within a moment, he was coming up the street toward the figure.

Since he was dressed in street clothes, he looked like any other person out for a late evening walk, and the shadowy figure didn't alter course as he got closer. But just as they got about six yards apart, the person must have seen it was Jared, and they darted down the alley next to Car's shop.

Jared gave chase, and I updated Tuck on their location. For a few moments, I stood holding my breath at the window until I saw Jared and Indie Radison coming out into the light on the street. "What in the world?" I said to Marcus and Rocky.

"Isn't that Car's niece?" Marcus said. "Why is she out, skulking about?"

I shook my head. "I guess we're going to find out." I wasn't surprised to see Jared bringing the young woman here since we were closing up and were closer than the police station. Indie wouldn't be arrested or anything just for being odd on the street, but I knew Jared would want to ask her a few questions.

I gave Tuck another update, and a moment later, I saw him park his truck across the street and jog over to meet Jared outside the shop. Marcus held the door open for the trio, and they all walked in, opting to come into the darkened café, I presumed, for a bit more privacy.

"Now, why did you run when you saw me, Indie?" Jared said after they let the woman sit down.

Marcus, Rocky, and I lingered nearby, trying to look like the pastry case needed the attention of three adult humans.

"I don't know," she said with a very affected shrug. "You scared me, is all."

"Oh yeah," Tuck said. "Why would a police officer be scary to you?"

"I didn't know he was a police officer. Just a man on the

street, and I was alone. That's scary, yeah?" She had a point, but I didn't believe that was her real reason.

"Why not run this way, then? Toward the bookstore? The lights were on, and you'd been here. Why go into a dark alley with a man behind you?" Tuck asked, clearly not buying her story either. "I mean, it's unfortunate that women have reason to fear men on the street, but if you were worried, wouldn't you have gone to the place you knew was safe?"

Indie deflated at this, which I presumed was because she knew her lie wouldn't hold up. "All right, fine. I was hoping to get into Uncle Car's shop and look around, see if there were any clues about what happened to Aunt Mildred there."

Jared shot me a look and tilted his head for me to come over. "You're trying to figure out who killed your aunt?" he asked as I joined them. "Why?"

She scowled up at him. "Because you're not doing anything. It's been days, and no one has been arrested." I heard the catch in her voice and realized she was trying not to cry.

"Were you and your aunt close?" I said as I pulled up a chair and sat down while also looking at the chairs in front of the two police officers to suggest they do the same.

Indie shook her head. "No, Mom didn't like her much, so I only saw her a few times in my life. But she sent me birthday cards with handwritten letters, and she always remembered me for graduation and such."

"She cared about you a lot," I said, not needing more confirmation than Indie's own impression. "So you care a lot about what happened to her?"

She sniffled. "Yeah, and I know you were worried about me looking into things, but I'm fine. I just wanted to get some answers. Why would someone kill her?"

Tuck tapped the table softly. "We want to know that, too, and I promise you, we are definitely looking into her murder.

Fervently," he added. "But I have to ask you, please, don't keep investigating." He looked over at me, and I nodded. "Indie, I've done what you're doing, and more than once, it's almost cost me my life. Take a note from me, and don't do it." A ping of inspiration hit me. "Instead, do you want to spend some time in the bookstore? Help us out for the holidays and hear the latest about the investigation whenever Tuck and Jared can share it?"

She sighed and looked at Tuck. "I have your word that you are actually investigating?"

"Absolutely," he said, "And as Harvey told you, we'll keep you updated as much as we can."

Indie put out her hand, and Tuck shook it formally. "All right, then," she said. "When can I start?"

"How about tomorrow?" I said. "You can help us get some more holiday decorations up and maybe staff the wrapping station if that suits you?" I wasn't sure why this young woman had time to hang out in our town, but if she needed something to keep her busy, this situation would be a win-win. After all, as good as Woody was with everything, I just didn't see wrapping gifts as his strong suit.

THE NEXT MORNING, Indie showed up right at ten, and I put her to work deciding how to display the evergreen swags and garlands that Elle had brought by. The pieces were simple branches of spruce interspersed with artemisia and dusty miller. Just enough silver to be festive without going overboard.

Indie went straight to work, and I was pleased to see she had a knack for decorating that was almost as strong as Marcus's visual eye. I smiled when she got into the windows and tastefully swagged the garland across the tops of each. It was just the touch the windows needed.

"That looks wonderful," I told her as she hopped down from the second window. "You have a knack."

She shrugged, but I saw a little color come into her cheeks. "I'm an interior designer most of the time," she said quietly. "So I can just kind of see things."

"What? You design house interiors? I didn't know that," I said.

She smiled. "There's a lot you don't know about me, Harvey. At least not yet."

I looked at her closely. "That's true, but I look forward to learning more. Whatever you want to share."

There was a sadness in her voice that seemed deep and dark, but as she had just said, we didn't know each other very well. I wasn't going to pry. "Feel like putting your expertise to work in the rest of the store?"

For a long time, I had relied on finds from vintage flea markets and thrift stores as my source for seating, and many of those items I still loved. And I definitely loved the eclectic feel of the store, but I also knew we needed to update in some ways. I just hadn't been able to determine how.

"Really? You'd let me do some design here?" Indie's face grew much brighter. "I'd love that." She spun slowly around. "Anything off limits?"

I shook my head. "Nope. I don't have a big budget for new things, but if you think of something you believe to be essential, I'll definitely consider it."

The new memberships were already bringing in added revenue. We just got our first online order from a member who visited a few days back. She wanted the full hardcover set of The First 100 Board Books, and I was glad to order it for her. She'd have it in a few days, all gift-wrapped and everything.

So if Indie found a few items we needed, I could afford to spiff up the place. Gracious, I loved running a business.

As my new designer headed farther into the shop, Jared

entered the front door with a wagon behind him. "The clocks are ready," he said as he steered the wagon over to the window. "We checked with Car, and he wanted them to come right back here. He's on his way over to help you put them back up."

I clapped my hands a couple of times. "Oh, yes. This day is going so well," I said and gave Jared a kiss on the cheek.

"Yeah?" he said with a small smile.

I told him about Indie and her design skills. "Now the clocks are back, and that feels like a victory, too." A thought occurred to me. "You didn't find anything helpful on them?"

He shook his head. "Not a thing." His phone pinged, and after he looked at it, he said, "Tuck needs another pair of eyes on something. I'll get the wagon later." He kissed my cheek and was out the door before I could ask what was up. I was sure that was entirely intentional.

As promised, Car came into the shop with Niall by his side a couple of minutes later. The two looked radiant, and their joy made mine even bigger.

"Hi, gentlemen," I said. "Thanks for coming to help. Mind if I recruit one more?"

"The more, the merrier," Car said as Niall helped him step into the window. "Shall I put them back where Marcus had them?"

I turned back from where I was halfway into the store and said, "You all do whatever you think looks best. Be right back." I jogged back to where Indie was strolling through the fiction section. "Want to help further snazzy up the windows while you ponder?"

She grinned. "Oh yeah, what have we got?"

I led her to the front of the store, and when she saw her uncle in the window, she positively beamed. "Uncle Car, can I help?"

Niall turned and grinned back at her as he put out his hand

to help her into the window with them. "Your skills are definitely needed," he said.

While I smiled at the happy trio in the window, I noticed the magazines were a wreck, so given that most people were browsing, I assigned myself the task of organizing them.

"So, where were these?" Niall asked from behind me.

Car cleared his throat. "The police had them. We found some notes in the backs of several that we thought might be linked to Mildred's murder."

Niall almost shouted, "What? What are you talking about?"

I turned to look at the three of them, and Niall looked visibly disturbed, Indie, too.

"Let's get these arranged," Car said, "And I'll show you my copies of the notes when we go get lunch." His eyes scanned the store and then landed on me. "That's okay, right?"

"Oh yeah," I said. "Maybe Niall and Indie will have some ideas."

Niall still looked stricken, but he nodded. And the three of them went back to arranging the display.

As they were finishing up, Marcus rolled into the store on his skateboard. He looked positively exuberant, and I guessed he was still riding the high of being newly engaged. I couldn't blame him. I'd practically bounced for two weeks after Jared proposed.

He kicked up his board as he came to a stop beside me. "The window is looking great."

I nodded. "Hope you don't mind that I recruited help?"

"No way. I like doing windows, but it's definitely not my favorite. Now, if you replaced me as assistant manager, we might need to talk."

I laughed. "Seriously, I could never replace you. Who would keep me on track?"

He laughed like a cartoon villain. "Ah, my plan is working."

His ride on his skateboard to the back room included a witch-like cackle.

I loved when everyone was in a good mood.

For the next couple of hours, Marcus and I did our usual bookstore thing, and by the end of the afternoon, the store was busy and subtly but noticeably more beautiful. Indie had gone to lunch with Niall and her uncle, and when she'd come back, she'd given me only a wave before delving into the world of interior design.

She started by switching some of the seating so that the most colorful chairs were in the front of the store, and then she began shifting the positions of each chair and side table just so. If I hadn't been watching her as I worked, I probably wouldn't have realized that she was moving every single piece of furniture, except the bookcases, which were screwed into the floor for security.

"How does that look?" she asked when she was done. "I wanted to make everything a little more vibrant and cozy."

I stared out across the space and smiled. "That's exactly what you've done. Did you have any more ideas?"

A corner of her mouth lifted. "Well, since you asked. Do you have a color printer?"

I nodded. "I do. Should I ask what you have in mind, or would you like to surprise me?"

"Oh, let me surprise you. I just need to run to the B&B for my laptop and pick up a couple of supplies on the way back. See you soon." She didn't even wait as she grabbed her coat from behind the register and jetted out the door.

I loved that enthusiasm, even though I had wanted to hear her thoughts on the notes in her uncle's clocks. I'd ask her later, I decided.

As my shift came to a close, I caught Marcus up on Indie's impending return and decided to take one last walk through the store, mostly to fill up my mind with what I might need to order the next day but also because I just loved my store. It was my favorite place.

I was heading to the front window where Taco and Mayhem had decided they wanted to be a part of the holiday display when Indie burst through the door and collapsed into one of the chairs she had just moved up before sobbing into her hands.

"What happened?" I said as I rushed over. "Are you okay?"

She shook her head and continued to cry into her arm. "I can't believe she was there," she said.

I knelt next to her and said, "Who was where?"

"Komiko. She was at my bed and breakfast." She took a long shuddering breath and looked up at me. "Sorry. You don't know who that is. Let's just say I had been hoping not to see her again."

"Oh, I know of Komiko," I said without even thinking. "She's a friend of your uncle's. Been in here a couple of times. She was at your aunt's funeral, too." For some reason, I kept talking even as Indie's face grew increasingly alarmed. "Seems like a nice woman."

"Nice woman?" Indie said with a huge breath behind her words. "You think she's nice?" She sat up and looked at the ceiling.

"Wait, you know her, and I don't. What's going on, Indie?" Something I had said had clearly disturbed her because she was now rubbing her hands against the back of her head in agitation. I put my hand on her knee. "Explain to me what I don't understand."

Indie glanced back down at me and let out a long breath. "Komiko and I went to school together over at MICA."

I nodded because I was familiar with the well-respected art school over in Baltimore.

"We were both in the design and architecture program. There weren't many of us that weren't 'fine,'"—she put air quotes around the word—"artists, so we got close quickly, even switched rooms so we could live together."

I nodded. At my small alma mater, we'd made friends with our dormmates and classmates super fast, too, partially because we needed people since we were on our own. "But clearly, your friendship didn't last?" I said.

"Didn't last is the gentle way to describe it. Imploded might be more accurate." She shook her head. "Suddenly, she was just gone for days on end, and when she'd come back from wherever she'd been, she wanted me to cover for her, to tell the Dean she'd been sick in our room."

I sighed because I could see where this was going.

"I did it the first couple of times, but she started disappearing so much that I felt like I wasn't helping her to lie. So I told our RD." She shook her head. "Komiko was furious."

I winced but then quickly said, "You did the right thing. She obviously needed help."

"That's what I said," Indie replied as she met my eyes for the first time since she came in. "I was just trying to help her. Something was definitely wrong. I thought it might be drugs." She took a hard breath.

"But it wasn't drugs?" I thought I already knew the answer, but it wasn't my place to say it.

"No, she was depressed. Going out for long walks that took her hours and hours away from campus." Indie shook her head. "When she finally talked to me about it, she said walking was the only way she thought she could say alive."

I felt the pain of that right in the center of my heart. "What happened?"

Indie sighed. "I'm not sure. She left school. That's all I really know."

I stood up because my knees were going to break in protest if I didn't. "And when you just saw her at the bed and breakfast? What happened?"

"She tried to hug me." Indie ran a hand over her face. "I'm not mad at her or anything, and I think we came to an understanding as roommates. But when she left, I carried a lot of guilt, and no one—not the dean, not our RD—would talk to me about it."

"Oh, that does sound hard. That was a lot to carry, I bet?"

She nodded. "I had to get some help with my own mental health after it all." She looked up at the front window. "I just hope Komiko got some, too."

"Did you talk to her at all? Just now, I mean?" It really wasn't my business, but since I knew Komiko had gotten help, I thought maybe she had shared that.

"No, I just ran out. I couldn't handle it, not with everything happening here." She looked at me. "Those notes, what did you make of them?"

I sighed. "Want to get some dinner?" I asked. "We can talk more about them."

"Yeah, I didn't even make it to my room for my laptop, and I still need to get—" she paused and gave me a small smile, "to get what I need for the surprise. Can I finish tomorrow?"

"Oh, of course," I said. "Let's go eat."

I texted Jared to let him know I wouldn't make it to his place as planned and told him I'd fill him in later. Then I took Indie's arm and steered her toward the best risotto I'd ever had.

Once Max had taken our orders, two mushroom risottos and a bottle of white wine, I asked her to tell me what she thought about the notes in her uncle's clocks. "Did you think they were relevant to your aunt's murder?"

Indie took a sip of wine. "I don't really know. I couldn't get a good sense of what the writer's intent was, you know? Part of me thought they were outright scary, and part of me"—she took another sip of wine—"part of me thought they were kind of sweet."

I nodded. "I know just what you mean. Where I'm stuck is

how they could possibly be relevant to your aunt's death. Aside from us finding them at about the same time, I can't see how they're linked."

Indie nodded. "I know what you mean."

"Did Car or Niall have any insights?" I asked as the server set our bowls of risotto and salads on the table.

"That's what was weird. Uncle Car was clearly stumped. He just kept reading the notes over and over again. But Niall seemed completely convinced the message didn't mean any harm." She ate a bite of her risotto. "Holy cow, this is good!"

"I know, right?" I said. "Okay, so did you get to see those funeral records I told you about?"

"Oh yeah, I meant to say thank you. Those were exactly what I think Aunt Mildred was trying to find." She grew quiet. "I just wish she'd known about them."

I was suddenly feeling like I was having dinner with a friend, and while I was wary of letting my guard down completely, it also felt good. "Me, too. Do you think she asked anyone for help?"

"Like who?" Indie asked as she prepared a perfect bite of salad.

I shook my head. "I don't know. She didn't go to the police, of course, but then she had no reason to. Maybe she hired a private detective?"

Indie groaned. "It would really help if we knew what she was trying to find. Was it simply that our family had a history of bipolar disorder? From what I read in her journal, it seemed like she already knew that. Maybe she just needed external proof?"

I sighed. "I don't know. But whatever she was looking into, it sure seemed like someone didn't want her to figure it out." I took another bite of my food and then said, "Did anyone tell you that your aunt was inside your uncle's building when she was killed?"

"What?" she said as she put her fork down. "No, I didn't know that." She looked out the window for a moment. "Did she have a key?"

"Car said he never gave her one." I looked down at my dish for a moment. "You didn't have one, did you? Your mom?"

Indie chewed her bite and shook her head. "No, we didn't come to see Uncle Car often enough to need one, and since Mildred was here, I doubt Mom would have even asked."

I sighed. "Well, then, I'm at a loss. Your uncle owns his building, I think, right?"

"Right," she said with a smile. "Who knew clockwork would be so lucrative, huh?"

I laughed. "Maybe we should have gone into that business." Her comment gave me pause, though. "A few years ago, buildings here were pretty cheap, but since St. Marin's has had a bit of a revival, I imagine his building was kind of pricy. Is he just really good with money?"

She studied me for a minute. "I have no idea, now that you say that. I just assumed he got a good deal, but I don't know why I'd think that. He may very well have a great deal of money. I have no concept." She looked across the street to where her uncle's shop was. "Now that you mention it, though, I am a bit puzzled about how he could afford such a nice place."

I followed her gaze. Car's building was two stories, like most of the buildings on Main Street, and I expected it was one of the older ones from the original town's street, given the way top architectural brickwork was done. It wouldn't have been cheap. "Maybe he took out a loan?"

Indie shrugged. "Maybe?" She studied my face a moment. "Still, it feels like we're maybe missing something, doesn't it?"

I nodded. "It does. And you know, in my experience, when it feels like we're missing something, it means we probably are. Maybe you could ask your uncle about the building? It might be a little less rude than if I asked."

"What, you think saying"—she cleared her throat and puffed out her chest—"'so, what did you pay for this here building, Car?'" she said in a deep voice, "might sound a little too bro-like."

I laughed. "Exactly. I don't know how men feel so comfortable talking about such things, but I certainly don't. I would be quite put off if someone asked me how much I paid for my shop."

"Well, now that you mention it, Harvey," Indie said in the same deep voice before she broke into a laugh that sounded like ringing bells.

I really liked this woman, and I hoped with all my heart that we could find who had hurt her aunt. Now, though, we had more pressing matters. "How do you feel about crème brûlée?" She smiled at me and tapped the back of her spoon on the table in the universal signal of affection from one *Amelie* fan to the other. "But only if it's good," she said.

I nodded vigorously. "Max's is just about as good as his risotto." Fortunately, I hadn't oversold the creamy dessert, and both Indie and I cleaned our ramekins.

10

The following morning, I woke up with a fluffy paw draped over my face. The fact that I had not noticed Aslan's passive-aggressive sleeping posture until daylight entered the room was a testament to just how tired and relaxed I had been when I got home.

Mart and I had watched a couple of episodes of the *Charmed* reboot without talking about anything except the snarky political references we loved in the show. And when I'd climbed into bed, I felt the calmest and most easy-going I had felt since we'd found that first note in Car's clock.

Upon waking, I was determined to stay in that calm place, so I carefully moved Aslan's paw to avoid disturbing the sleeping lioness and headed into the kitchen for coffee. Mart had beat me to it, and while I poured myself a cup, she caught me up on the property the winery was hoping to buy. It was a mountaintop near Charlottesville and where Jared had proposed when we had recently visited.

"I may need to visit there often, and of course, I'll need someone to split the driving," she said with a wink.

"Absolutely. Of course you will, and I believe I'll need to

scope out some of the new bookstores out there just to see what the latest trends in the business are." I was enjoying the thought already. Now that Woody was around to split shifts with Marcus, I could take more time off, and I was looking forward to that. "Business expenses all the way."

Mart gave me a high five on the way out the front door. "I have an early day. Meet you at the store to plan for the bazaar?"

I nodded. Mart was going to be serving wine in the café again, as she did at most of the events we had. We'd even gotten our liquor license so that she could advertise the winery's presence at the shop without running afoul of regulators. Between her wine offerings and the special liquor-infused drinks that Stephen and Rocky had created, our guests had a lovely addition to their evenings at the shop.

Plus, since we put a two-drink limit on everyone who came in by issuing tickets when we checked ID, we didn't compete with Max's full bar or the other alcohol vendors in town. In fact, Max had said our new drink offerings actually meant he got more business because people had a couple of drinks at our place and then wandered down to his to continue the celebration.

Today, Mart and I were deciding the schedule for the winery, and she was going to bring the winery's new prosecco offering to see if we might want to start the day with mimosas. I was never one to turn down mimosas, and I was fairly sure that was going to be an easy yes on my part. But if I had to sample some wine, I could do that. You know, for the business.

Unfortunately, the lift in my spirits that a sip of wine and orange juice had promised was short-lived because when Taco, Mayhem, and I got to work, Malaysia was outside waiting for us, and she didn't look happy. In fact, she strode toward me so intensely as I came up the street that both Mayhem and Taco stopped walking, locked their legs, and growled at her. These two rarely growled at anyone, but today, they weren't holding back.

"Tame your mutts," Malaysia shouted as Mayhem began to bark.

I took a deep breath, spoke to Mayhem to ask her to be quiet, and then looked at Malaysia. "Can I help you, Malaysia?"

"Yes, you can stop talking to my daughter." Her tone was sharp, and Mayhem began to growl again. Taco took a step closer to the woman.

"You want me to stop talking to Indie? Why is that?" I wanted to sound reasonable and calm, but this woman had basically accosted me on the street on a lovely winter morning. I wasn't in the mood. "She's a grown woman, and I would wager she's quite able to make her own decisions about who she speaks to."

Malaysia's face went a sort of green-red color that was actually fitting for the season, even if it was a little disturbing on a human face, and she raised her voice loud enough that people up the street turned. "You will do as I ask, or I will get the authorities involved."

Now I had to suppress a smile because, well, she had no grounds for whatever she was accusing me of and because I was engaged to one police officer and good friends with the other. Not that they wouldn't do their jobs if I had committed a crime, but they certainly weren't going to be inclined to take the rantings of a woman on a sidewalk seriously.

I stared at Malaysia for a minute as I took a few more deep breaths, and just when I was about to ask her if she'd like to come inside to talk—I could see Marcus coming up the street, so I knew we wouldn't be alone inside—Car came walking quickly across the street.

"Malaysia, what are you doing?" he said as he stepped onto the concrete beside us. "You are making quite the scene."

I looked from brother to sister, and as I watched, Malaysia deflated from her bluster. "I'm sorry, Car," she said.

"It's not me you need to apologize to," he said firmly.

Malaysia looked over at me and glared. Clearly, an apology wasn't coming my way anytime soon.

I smiled back at her, refusing to do what a younger me would have done—brush off the attack with a "don't worry about it" or some such. Instead, I just waited until the silence became more uncomfortable for her than for me.

At that point, she mumbled something that sounded vaguely like an apology.

I squelched my instinct to say, "What was that?" And instead said, "Let's go inside to talk, okay?"

Marcus gave me a serious look as he rolled up. "Everything okay here?" he asked as he took out his keys.

"Not really," I said, "but we'll figure it out. Can you handle opening up?"

"Of course," he said before looking right past Malaysia, who was still glowering at me, and said, "Good morning, Car."

"Morning, Marcus," Car said and shook his hand before following him inside.

I waited a moment while Malaysia considered her options before finally turning to proceed after her brother. I gave the dogs lots of "Good pups" and ear scratches before we followed everyone into the store.

After releasing the hounds and finding they wanted to stay with me rather than head to their beds as they usually did, I walked over to where Car and Malaysia had taken seats in the café. Rocky was preparing the coffee for the morning, and when I walked over, I said, "If you could, would you please bring over three mugs of your freshest for us when they're ready? I, at least, need the caffeine."

"You okay?" she asked.

"I am, but stay close, okay? I may need to be restrained." I was only half joking.

"Gotcha," she said. "Do I need to bring rope?"

"Only if I want to strangle someone," I said as I turned to head back to the table. "So maybe?" I smiled but then rolled my eyes. I wasn't in the mood for this conversation, but I also knew that tension like this didn't just go away. So I sat down and said, "What seems to be the issue, Malaysia?"

"You need to stop putting crazy, dangerous ideas in my daughter's head," she said.

Car put up a hand. "Let's not use the word *crazy*, all right. It's insulting to people who struggle with mental illness." His voice was soft but forceful in a way I had not heard before.

His sister looked at him and nodded. "Sorry," she said to him before turning back to me. "Indie thinks she can figure out who killed our sister, and she says you gave her the idea at dinner."

I shook my head. "Actually, I've warned Indie twice now about getting involved in a murder investigation. I thought she was backing off?"

Malaysia frowned. "You warned her?"

I nodded. "But that doesn't mean she listened. What did she say she was going to do?"

"She just keeps talking about Mildred's research and how it must be a clue." Malaysia's jaw clenched. "She gets like this sometimes. Just won't let something go."

I glanced over at Car, and he was studying his sister's face with careful concern. I gave it a minute to see if he wanted to say anything, but when he didn't, I said, "Her aunt was murdered. That's a hard thing to let go." I wanted to add that it was hard to just "get over" the murder of anyone, something I knew from experience, but I wanted to stay focused on the topic at hand.

Malaysia sighed. "I know that, but why does she have to be

the one to look into it? It was probably just some vagrant passing through the area. Maybe she told him to get cleaned up, and he didn't like it."

I furrowed my brow and said, "That's a very specific theory, especially for a town that has made a concerted effort to make housing available for most people struggling with homelessness." My mom had been a major part of spearheading that effort a year or so ago, and now we had multiple low-income rental units available, plus a couple of affordable houses built for particular families, too.

"It happens all the time," Malaysia said with emphasis. "St. Marin's isn't paradise, you know."

"Oh, I know," I said, "but fortunately, homelessness isn't one of the struggles we have." I really had a lot more to say on this subject, but instead, I decided to explore a question I had, even though I was sure Jared and Tuck had already found an answer. "Besides, a person living with homelessness wouldn't have had a key to Car's building, so they couldn't have left Mildred's body there."

Car winced, and I regretted my less-than-gentle choice of words.

I looked over at Malaysia, and she was staring out the front window. "That's true," she said, "unless, of course, Car, you were as free with your keys as you were when you lived in the other half of my duplex." The venom in her words was fierce and even more intense than the vitriol she'd spilled at me on the sidewalk.

Car blanched. "I have apologized for those, er, poor choices on more than one occasion, Malaysia. I thought we were past this."

I was not feeling uncomfortable. Clearly, this was some family history that was quite raw still, and while I didn't really want to be there while they poked at old wounds, I could neither think of a way to gracefully extricate myself nor let go of the distinct feeling I had that this moment was really important. So, I just stayed quiet.

"Well, for all I know, you're having one of your episodes again—" she started to say.

"Malaysia Radison, how dare you imply that I am not caring for my health or that I wouldn't be seeking help if I couldn't do so? How dare you?" Car was furious, and for the first time since I'd met him, he raised his voice, and quite loudly, too.

Malaysia waved a hand as if she had just brought up her brother's love of acid-washed jeans instead of implying that he wasn't mentally stable. "Well, did you?"

"No," Car said. "The only people who have keys are Elle at the farm stand—just so a neighbor had one—and you." He stared at his sister for a long moment before glancing over at me, almost as if he'd forgotten I was there. "Apologies, Harvey."

I decided to pretend like I hadn't heard most of that conversation and said, "So only Malaysia and Elle have keys? You've told Tuck?"

Car nodded. "I believe they've spoken with both of them." He looked over at Malaysia, "Correct?"

"It was humiliating to be accused of killing your own sister." She rested her forehead in her hands. "They knew I wasn't even in town that night when you all went to dinner. Ridiculous."

This wasn't the same sweet spiritual woman I'd met a couple of days ago. That woman I had liked, but this one, this one I could do without. I wondered which one was genuine or maybe both were. I'd certainly known enough people in my life who could be one person in a certain situation and another entirely in a different scenario.

"It's always hard to be a suspect," I said, speaking from experience. It had been really hard, but I also understood why I had been suspected. It was even harder when my dad was a suspect, but even then, we'd all wanted justice. It didn't seem like Malaysia cared much about who had killed her sister at all. Then again, I obviously didn't know the first thing about this woman and her emotions. For all I knew, she grieved by shouting at people.

Car stood and looked at me as he put a gentle handle under his sister's arm to help her up, too. "Thank you for your time, Harvey. We'll be going now."

"Sure thing, Car, and please, if you need anything, let me know, okay?"

"Thank you, Harvey," he said and practically pulled his sister out the front door. She wasn't actually saying anything, but from the look on her face, I got a distinct impression she was definitely sharing some choice words with me mentally.

I returned to the register to fill Marcus in on what had just happened.

"So she wants to keep her grown daughter from looking into the research her aunt was doing? Talk about controlling," he said.

I nodded. "Malaysia obviously doesn't have a clear sense of other people's boundaries." I shook my head. "But what's bothering me is that Indie seemed quite content to continue her aunt's research and leave the police investigation to the police. But maybe I was wrong?"

"Easy enough to check if you have her number," Marcus said.

"True," I said. "I'll be right back." I stepped into our back room to give her a call. This kind of situation required conversation, not just an exchange of texts. "Sorry to bother you," I said when we had exchanged the usual pleasantries. "Your mom just came by and was concerned that you were in danger because you were looking into your aunt's murder."

"My mother is too caught up in her own head sometimes. I told her that I was continuing Aunt Mildred's research into bipolar disorder, and she sort of lost it, said she didn't want me dredging up long-buried secrets." Indie's voice sounded weary. "She must have gotten herself all worked up thinking that would mean I could come afoul of the murderer."

I smiled to myself. My mother had once been the overly involved type, so I understood. "Okay, good. I hope you don't think I'm overstepping. She was just really upset, and I wanted to let you know."

"Thanks, Harvey. I hope she wasn't too much trouble. I'll have a word with her if she's crossed a line." I wondered how many times Indie had needed to do that previously.

"Oh no, it's fine. Your uncle was here, too, and I think they're probably talking about things," I said as I tried to smooth things over for my friend and avoid another intense encounter with her mother.

"Great. I'm walking up now for my shift. See you in a minute," she said.

"Awesome. See you soon." I hung up and made my way back out onto the floor just in time for us to open. I gave Marcus a thumbs-up as I headed to the front of the shop, flipped on our neon sign, and unlocked the door. Something besides the obvious ugly tone in my conversation with Malaysia wasn't sitting right with me, but I couldn't quite tease out what was bothering me.

And I didn't have time to think about it for most of the day. We were swamped with holiday shoppers, and Indie's talent for ribbons delighted everyone who asked for gift wrapping. Plus, she was charming with the customers, especially the children, who she taught to curl a ribbon and tie elaborate bows to take home. At one point, when she'd just given out eight bows, she looked at me and asked if she should stop with the free ribbons. "I don't want to break your wrapping budget."

"Are you kidding?" I said. "Those kids will always remember this bookstore because of you. That is priceless . . . for them and me."

She grinned at that and stepped up her wrapping game to make her work even more gorgeous. If she hadn't already been an interior designer, she could definitely start a business as a professional gift wrapper. I didn't know if that was even a thing, but Indie could make it one if it wasn't.

When I was staffing the register for the fairly constant stream of customers, I had a great time recommending a "honeymooner's book basket" assortment for the bridal party of a couple getting married in St. Marin's that weekend. The couple were bibliophiles, but one of the brides was an especially avid reader. So her bridal party wanted an assortment of books she could read on her Irish holiday honeymoon and also enjoy talking about with her new wife.

I recommended all light and fun titles, including *The Storied Life of A.J. Fikry* because it was all about books and romance, and then I suggested the Outlander series because while both of these betrothed were lasses, I suspected they might still relish the romance—and the great sex scenes—between Claire and Jamie.

When the wedding party left, they had twenty-five books, an assortment of pastries for breakfast the next morning, and the most gorgeously decorated gift basket I had ever seen, courtesy of Indie, of course. I was going to have to think about marketing both the basket and Indie's wrapping ideas.

Later that morning, Mart came by with the new prosecco, and all of us on staff had a taste—just for the sake of different palates, of course—and every person agreed it was delicious and would be a great addition to the weekend's fare for the bazaar. Even Stephen and Walter, who were staffing a table for the membership program again and were, by far, the most discerning drinkers I'd ever known, loved it and placed their New Year's Eve order right then and there as Mart scrambled to find a piece of paper.

Just as I began to feel the day's fatigue sink in, Komiko

slipped quietly into the shop. I thought she had probably hoped to just wander into the back of the store without drawing attention to herself, but given how awkward her last visit had been, I wanted to be sure to speak to her to see if I could put her a little more at ease.

So, I took a roundabout route and met up with her where she was browsing the cookbooks. "Can I help you find anything in particular?" I said.

The poor woman spun so fast that I thought she might fall over. "Oh, Harvey, you scared me," she said. "No, I'm honestly just looking for an excuse to be here."

I tilted my head.

"In your store, I mean," she said quickly. "It's just so peaceful here."

I smiled. "Oh, I'm glad you still think so. Your last visit was a little, well—"

She interrupted me. "Weird. It was weird. I didn't know that Indie was Car's niece, and apparently, they didn't realize we all knew each other."

"Sure, that was certainly part of what was weird." Again, it wasn't my place to talk about her past with Indie, but I did think it weird, for lack of a better word, that Komiko wouldn't realize how, even a decade later, that kind of thing might leave a little tension in any relationship.

She nodded. "I hope I get to see them again," she said, "so I can try to explain."

I swallowed because I wasn't really sure how sincere Komiko was about that desire. Still, it was probably better she knew Indie was here than be blindsided again. "Indie's actually up the front wrapping gifts . . . you know, if you want to speak to her."

Komiko's already very fair skin went a more profound shade of white and confirmed my suspicion that she didn't really want to see her old roommate. But then again, she was still in town, and if she knew both Car and Indie were here, why not just go home? People were so odd sometimes.

The young woman stared at me, and I watched a variety of emotions flash across her face—fear, maybe anger, and then a quiet kind of resolve. "Okay, but could you stay with me? At least until I see how things go?"

I nodded. So many times in my life, I had wanted to ask a friend to be nearby for hard conversations, but something about how we think adults are supposed to function made me disinclined to ask for help. Komiko was quite brave to ask for what she needed.

The two of us walked up to where Indie was refilling her wrapping supplies, and Indie smiled.

"Hi, Komiko," she said.

"Hi," Komiko responded. "I wanted to tell you I was sorry for the other day." She cleared her throat. "And for back in college, too. I've had a hard few years, and I'm sorry they affected you."

"Well, thank you for apologizing. I hope you know that you can ask me if you ever need help. I'm your friend." Indie reached out and hugged her friend.

These two women were impressive in their maturity. I wasn't nearly as far along in my own understanding of humanity at their age as they were. "I'll take care of wrapping for a while if you guys want to go hang out in the café or something," I said.

"Buy you coffee?" Indie asked.

Komiko smiled. "Yep, but I only do decaf. That's part of what I need to tell you."

"You won't even know Rocky's decaf is decaf," Indie said as she slipped her arm through Komiko's.

I watched the two of them walk away and felt a little twist of relief in my chest. At least some healing was coming out of all this.

The afternoon continued with customers coming in steadily, and even when Indie returned to wrapping, a bright smile on her face, we were both steadily busy with customers. Marcus was staffing the floor and was definitely getting his ten thousand steps in.

Just before it was time for me to end my shift, the door opened to Car and Niall, hand in hand. The two men smiled at me and headed my way. "Harvey, we want to ask you a favor. Would you mind if we held a small gathering in your reading area tomorrow?"

"Of course not." I studied their faces. "What can we do to help with prep?"

"Nothing at all," Niall said. "But if you can stop by, we'd love to have you there."

"Absolutely," I said, even as I squelched my desire to ask a lot of nosy questions. "The bazaar starts tomorrow, so the store might be hopping, but we have plenty of room. Maybe the holiday energy will add to your gathering."

"No doubt about that," Car said as he winked at me. "Could you invite the rest of the staff to stop over, too?"

"Sure," I said. We set up the final details of what tables and chairs they needed and the start time, and the two men left, still holding hands. They were everything.

WHILE I DID EXTRICATE myself from the shop at five, leaving Indie and Marcus to run the shop, I wasn't quite done with work. I needed to finish up a few things for the bazaar the next day, including doing some last-minute social media posts, such as filling our Instagram stories with Galen's posts about the shop. He'd been on fire this week.

So while Jared made beer bread to go with the beef stew he'd had in the crockpot all day, I sat at the dining room table, putting up posts and checking emails. It was then that a message from Niall Baker popped into the store inbox. It was addressed to the All Booked Up Staff, and I whooped with delight when I saw that it was an invitation to their engagement party at my store the next day.

"They're getting married," I shouted to Jared.

He walked in, a ladle in his hand. "Who?"

"Car and Niall." I told them about their afternoon visit and then showed him the invitation.

"Oh, that's great," he said just as his phone dinged in his pocket. "Looks like the department was invited, too." He showed me a text message from Tuck with the invitation.

I clapped my hands in delight. "Oh no, but I don't have a gift."

Jared walked back to the kitchen and quickly returned with a cutting board and a loaf of steaming bread. "Given the short notice, I expect they don't want gifts, but why don't you make a donation to the Mental Health Association in their honor? A gift from the store?"

"Oh, that's a great idea," I said. "I'll suggest that to other folks, too." I glanced at the electronic invitation to see who else had been invited and saw all of our friends there and my parents. This wasn't going to be such a small gathering after all.

Quickly, I sent off a text to everyone with Jared's suggestion about the donations, and almost immediately, the flurry of responses was full of agreement and a suggestion that we put together a gift box from the things we all created. Soon, we had tickets to the Maritime Museum from Lucas, pieces of art from Cate and Henri, a spice rack from Woody, jams and jellies from Elle, a custom drink mixed by Stephen and Walter, a dinner for two at Max's from Mom and Dad, a month's worth of coffee from Rocky, and a large assortment of wedding books from Marcus and me. It was a lovely gift, and it would be a delight to give it to them tomorrow.

11

Marcus and I had decided to open the store early for the first day of the bazaar, and while we talked about nine, I was glad we'd decided to try for eight. By the time we opened the doors, Main Street was already full with folks out for the early holiday farmer's market that Elle had coordinated and for early visits with Santa on his first full day in residence in St. Marin's.

The bookstore and coffee shop made a great stopover for folks making a day of it in town, and we had our fair share of holiday shoppers buying gifts for other folks, too. When our usual opening time rolled around, I'd already sold two huge coffee table books—Gray Malin's beautiful and whimsical photograph collection and a collection of Sendak's remarkable art. Since I typically sold one of those expensive types of books once a month, this was a huge boon and compensated for all the returns I had to make of books that were damaged by my casual browsing policy.

Those sales, combined with the steady stream of folks stopping by and staying at Stephen and Walter's table, which they had insisted on running all day today, meant we would have a great day. Indie arrived at nine to a line of folks waiting for her gift-wrapping expertise, and since some people had even brought in gifts they'd brought at other stores, Marcus and I decided we needed to do something to offset those costs. We opted to ask for a five-dollar donation to the Mental Health Association for every patron who brought an outside gift. Since people gave far more than five dollars when they brought in a gift to be wrapped, I had to empty the jar long before noon. At that point, we had already raised five hundred dollars, which would be a great addition to the donation Marcus and I were planning to make in Car and Niall's honor.

Niall and Car came in around noon and, after we enthusiastically congratulated them, headed to the reading area to set up for the reception with Marcus close at hand if they needed anything. Mom and Dad had come in that morning and set up the space as the men had requested, so I hoped the grooms would only have to do a bit to personalize the space the way they wished.

When Lu came in with warming trays full of her delicious food, I knew everything was in good hands. She would ensure the space looked gorgeous and the food was easily accessible. I struggled with those things myself, but Lu always picked up the slack when I couldn't figure out table arrangement or crowd flow.

We had a brief lull in sales, and I snuck back to the supply room to compile the gifts our friends had been bringing by all morning. The basket Elle had brought to hold everything was enormous, but I still had to tape most of the gift cards and certificates to the outside of the basket to avoid crushing them beneath all the other goodies inside.

At one p.m., the reading space was full of well-wishers, and Rocky asked Maybelle to watch the café. Marcus and I hung near the entrance to the reading space and sipped champagne so we could enjoy the party while keeping an eye on the store.

Whenever we saw a customer needing help, we'd alternate slipping away to help. It was a good way to keep up the great sales day and enjoy the celebration, too.

The party began with a few words from the grooms. Car went first. "When I met Niall almost twenty-five years ago, I didn't like him very much." A chuckle passed around the space. "But then he wooed me with flowers, chocolates, and even songs on the sidewalk outside my house. He came pretty close to becoming Romeo to my, er, Romeo."

As Car continued, he told a classic love story, one where the two people got to know one another and slowly, over time, found they didn't want to spend a single day without one another. By the time Car was done speaking, I was teary, a situation that was exacerbated when Jared came and took my hand.

Fortunately, Niall was a natural comic, which we discovered when he began his speech. "Now, it's my turn to tell you the actual story. Carson Radison was head over heels from the first time he saw me in my sweatpants at the local coffee shop in Baltimore. I'm not sure if it was the tube socks with sandals or the extravagant bedhead, but from that moment on, he was certain I was the one for him."

Niall's speech ended with such reverence for his fiancé that it was almost a prayer. "Car, I can't believe it took nine proposals, including one heinously botched one, to get you to say yes, but I'm ever so glad you did."

The crowd applauded when the speech was finished, and the men kissed. For the rest of the afternoon, the guests milled around eating and sometimes shopping, but mostly celebrating the love that came, even if late in life.

When the crowd began to disperse, it was almost six o'clock, and I was exhausted. Marcus suggested that he finish the night and sleep in, and I readily agreed. I rarely slept late, but I could certainly go to bed early without any trouble.

Jared and I were leashing up the dogs at the same moment

Car and Niall were headed out. "Mind if I ask them to come over for soup?" Jared whispered to me. "I'm dying to hear about the nine proposals."

"That's a great idea," I said and smiled when the couple said they'd be delighted.

The six of us walked over to Jared's, with Niall taking great delight in the antics of Mayhem and Taco, who were, of course, putting on quite the show of getting their leads tangled and peeing with extensive extravagance.

When we arrived, I went inside to make a very simple but delicious batch of canned tomato soup that I doctored with fresh basil and oregano from the big herb garden on the back deck in Jared's new greenhouse. I'd bought it for him as an early holiday present since he wanted to do some year-round gardening, and I was thrilled to find my gift benefited me, too.

Soon, the men came in, and I served the soup with grilled cheese sandwiches made with Havarti and cheddar, a simple but delicious meal made even better with great company and amazing stories. Niall and Car had met in a coffee shop, and Niall had been in torn sweats with bedhead, but Niall had immediately fallen for Car.

"I just wasn't in a place to date at that point," Car said. "I had just come out of the hospital for the first time, and coping with everyday life was hard enough without adding someone else to it." He glanced over at Niall with affection. "If I had known how much better Niall would make my life, though, how well he could love me even when I was ill, I would have proposed to him on the spot."

It had, indeed, taken Niall eight proposals and twenty-five years to get his love to believe that he wasn't backing away because of Car's illness. "This last time, though," Niall said with a laugh, "he barely waited for me to finish the question before he said yes."

"I knew I couldn't live without him, and I finally believed he felt the same way about me. And I could imagine our life here so easily," Car added. "It was a very easy yes this time."

They were so beautiful together, and I loved that they would be a part of our community now. I did have one more question, though. "I thought there were nine proposals?" Niall and Car both blushed. "Oh yes, for you, that's the most important one," Car said. "Remember the notes in the clock?"

I looked from him to Niall and then back to Car. "Those were a proposal?"

"What?" Jared added.

"Yep," Niall said as his cheeks reddened further. "In retrospect, it was a bad idea because of both their placement and the cryptic code." He sighed. "I actually put them there in late October when I visited."

"But I didn't do my usual cleaning this year. I was too busy with repairs and sales," Car said. "So Marcus had the misfortune of finding them." He chuckled nervously.

But I didn't hold back and broke out into a full laugh. "That is the best news," I said as I grabbed Jared's hand. "We solved a mystery without anyone being in danger."

My fiancé laughed too. "I wish they were all that simple."

The mood sobered, and Car looked at Jared. "No more direction on my sister's murder."

Jared shook his head. "We are still following every lead, but right now, we're a little stymied, I have to say." He let out a hard breath. "You haven't thought of anything new by any chance, have you?"

Car shook his head. "I've been racking my brain, especially since Malaysia made such a big deal this morning about my tendency to give out keys, but I even checked my receipt. I only had three keys made, and I have one, Malaysia has one, and Elle has one."

"What's this about Malaysia?" Jared asked.

"Oh, Harvey hasn't told you?" Car said. "Sorry."

"It's fine. I just haven't had a chance to catch Jared up on my day." I told him quickly about the incident with Malaysia at the store but let Car share her suspicions that he had given a key to someone who had killed Mildred.

Jared nodded as he finished. "If it helps, you can give me a copy of that receipt for the official file. I don't need it for the investigation, but I could show it to your sister if she asks."

"I'll do that," Car said. "Sometimes, I need backup with my sisters—I mean, sister. Both of them want so badly to take care of me."

I stared at Car and felt a deep well of sympathy for him. Not only did he feel like he couldn't trust himself or his memory to know what he had or hadn't done, but his sister didn't trust him either. That made me very sad, and I didn't know what to say.

So, I got up and brought dessert out, a plate of Ghirardelli chocolate squares that I had stashed away for emergencies. It was a very basic dessert, but everyone seemed to appreciate it. We talked for a bit longer, mostly about the bazaar and the events, and then the guys headed out to walk back to town.

I stuck around long enough to help Jared clean up and then snuggle a bit, but I wanted to sleep in my own bed that night, especially since I had to be up so early, far earlier than Jared, in the morning.

"Night," he told me from the door. "Text me when you get home."

"Of course," I said and headed out with the two dogs for a quick walk home in the cold.

Mayhem and Taco must have been feeling the cold, too, because they moved along at quite a clip. We were just coming down our block when they both stopped short and started to growl. It wasn't unusual for a possum or raccoon to be prowling about, and while my pups were far more afraid of wild animals than the wild was afraid of them, they often acted as if they were guarding me against a serial killer.

I was tired, though, and I just wanted to get into my bed and go to sleep. So, I pushed the dogs onward as they growled more and more fiercely. "Guys, quiet. It's just a possum or a cat." I briefly wondered if Aslan had gotten out and was waiting on the stoop.

But once I got closer to the house, I saw why the dogs were so riled up. Malaysia was standing there on my stoop, and she looked furious. I started to put my gloved hand into my pocket to take out my phone, but her voice stopped me.

"I wouldn't do that, Harvey," she said. "I've already lost control once recently. I might just do it again."

I was still about a quarter of a block away, so I couldn't quite see all of her body with the porch light on behind her. It wasn't until I got a few steps closer that I noticed the pistol in her hand. "Oh," I said quietly.

"That's right. I need you to listen to me. My brother won't be here to deter me this time. You have to tell Indie to stop her research, all of it." She waved the gun at me like it was a scolding finger.

I took a deep breath and walked a couple of steps closer, holding tight to the dogs' leashes so that they didn't get shot. "I did talk to her earlier today, Malaysia. I reiterated that it was dangerous for her to look into her aunt's murder." I was scared for sure, but I was also angry. What was this woman's problem?

Malaysia shook her head and pointed the gun more directly at my head. "No, you don't understand me. She needs to stop researching altogether. She's going to find out things she doesn't need to know."

I paused for a moment and tried to think. So this wasn't just about Mildred's murder then. My brain was spinning fast, but I couldn't put all the pieces together with a gun in my face. "Can we go inside? You can explain this to me so I can be sure to tell Indie the right thing this time?" Despite my fear, the cold was starting to get to me, and I imagined Malaysia might have been waiting a long time for me. She had to be cold, too.

She stared at my face for a long moment. "Okay," she said. "But you have to listen this time."

"I will," I said and motioned toward the door. "The dogs might do better if I go in first."

She glanced at Mayhem, who was baring her teeth now. "Okay. But don't try anything." I nodded and steered the dogs around her before I unlocked the door and let them in. Malaysia came in behind me and slammed the door shut without turning her gun from my body. The dogs growled again but a little less intensely this time.

"If you put that away, they'll probably calm down. I can feed them and light a fire. They might settle then." I was still holding their leashes tight to make it seem like they were straining, even though the fact that I had invited Malaysia in had calmed them quite a bit.

"Okay," she said. After a second, she put her hand and the gun into her coat pocket.

I nodded and then walked the pups to the kitchen and pulled out the container of food. Quickly, I fed them both in Mayhem's bowl, something I never did since Taco was a food fiend, and then I walked into the living room to light a fire. The logs were already stacked, so I just had to tuck in some newspaper from the basket next to the hearth and strike a match to get it going.

Finally, I turned on the lamp by the front window and sat down. It had all taken less than two minutes, but Malaysia was tapping her foot the whole time. Now she sat in the armchair opposite me and said, "You ready to listen?"

"I am," I said, even as I continued to try to formulate a theory for what exactly was going on.

As I'd said they would, Mayhem and Taco came and lay on

their beds by the fire, but they didn't become less vigilant. Instead, they perched their heads on their paws and stared at Malaysia. I had no doubt that if that gun came out again or she made any movement toward me, they'd be on their feet and between her and me in a moment. But I wasn't about to let them get shot. No way.

"I want you to call Indie and tell her that it's a bad idea for her to look into what her aunt was researching. You can tell her that you think that's what got Mildred killed and that it's probably dangerous." Malaysia had clearly been thinking about this plan all day.

"Okay, I can do that," I said. "But we have to make it convincing so she'll believe me. What else should I say?"

Malaysia tilted her head and seemed to be considering. I just had to keep her talking for a bit longer. Just a bit longer.

"What if you tell her that you think her aunt was unwell— you know, mentally—that you've done some more digging and think that whatever she was trying to figure out was all in her head?" Malaysia said with a nod.

"You think that will convince her?" I asked.

Malaysia nodded more fervently this time. "I think so." She looked at me sharply. "If you sell it, really make her believe you're worried."

Oh, I'm worried, I thought, but I just nodded along with the woman in my armchair. "Okay, I can do that." I pointed to my pocket. "My phone is in here. I can call her right now. You can listen."

"Okay, that's a good idea," she said. "Let's do that." She was sitting back now, a bit more relaxed. I just needed her to take her hand out of her pocket and away from that gun.

I very slowly slipped my hand into my coat pocket and took out my phone. Then I stared at the screen as I scrolled through my contacts before tapping and letting the phone dial. "Hi, Indie?" I said.

Malaysia nodded and relaxed further in the chair, folding her arms across her chest.

"Yes, it's Harvey again. So I've been thinking about the conversation you and I had this morning about your Aunt Mildred's research," I continued. "I don't think she was really going anywhere with that, do you? I mean, maybe she wasn't feeling well herself. Maybe she was a little paranoid or something," I suggested.

I waited a moment for the person on the other end of the line to finish speaking, and then I said, "Right. So maybe it would be better for you to keep on with your business in Baltimore and go back to interior design. I bet your mom would even love to spend more time with you."

Malaysia actually smiled at this, so I played it up, even as the voice on the other end of the line urged calm.

"Maybe your mom could help you with your business, even. She seems like a woman with some great management skills. Do you need someone to run your office or anything?"

The call's recipient said a couple of things, to which I nodded and smiled for Malaysia's benefit.

"Exactly. Then you'd get more time with her and more help for yourself. Imagine how successful your business could be with two smart women at the helm," I said with as much energy as I could divert from keeping myself and my dogs alive.

On the other end of the line, I heard Jared say, "Okay, Harvey, now!"

I dove across the floor and lay down over the dogs just as the front and back doors to my house flung open, and Jared and Tuck charged in with their guns drawn.

Malaysia didn't have time to draw her own weapon before she faced two armed police officers. "In her left pocket," I shouted from where I was still sheltering the dogs by the fireplace.

Tuck quickly disarmed her and had her cuffed in a matter of seconds. Then Jared ran over to me to see if I was okay. "I'm fine," I said as my voice quivered. "Physically, at least." I lay down between the pups. "I think I'll just rest here, though." Mayhem propped her head on my chest, and Taco rolled over on his side with his back against me. I would take all the comfort I could get.

12

The next day, as Jared, Mart, and I sat around the kitchen island and ate copious amounts of bacon while sharing generously with the two hounds beside us, I was still feeling tired but also a little giddy. Mildred's murder was solved—at least, it appeared that way.

On the way to Tuck's patrol car, Malaysia had been yammering away about how so many women didn't know how to mind their own business, including her sister. "If they all just stayed out of family secrets, no one would have had any trouble, but no, Mildred never could just let things be. She always had to know more, always had to be in charge."

It wasn't quite a confession, but it seemed likely that Malaysia had killed her sister. They'd be comparing her hands to the strangle marks on Mildred's neck to see if they were a match, and Tuck was hopeful that evidence might convince Malaysia to confess.

For now, though, Jared was focused on something else. "Harvey, I told you to jump behind the couch, not jump in front of the dogs," he said with a shake of his head. "What if she had managed to pull the gun?"

I shrugged. "My body is bigger than theirs, so I had more chance of being wounded instead of killed than they did. I made a calculated choice."

Mart groaned. "Seriously, Harvey. They're amazing dogs, but you can't risk your life for them."

Taco moaned from beside her feet.

"I think a certain basset hound disagrees," I said.

DESPITE MY STRESSFUL NIGHT, I was still determined to open the shop early, and since the incident with Malaysia had, somehow, not become town news yet, I was able to do so in relative peace with my canine and police deputy guards nearby. Jared was off for the day, so he decided he would help me in the store.

"Because you had a rough night," he said, which was true, but I also knew he just needed to be close for his own sake. I didn't mind.

The rest of our friends would know the situation soon enough, and I was glad to see that Marcus wasn't in when I got there. He needed some rest too, and of course, since he had closed the night before, the shop was immaculate.

Given that we'd sold a bunch of our mystery books already, I asked Jared if he'd mind wrapping up a few more after I grabbed them off the shelf, and soon, he was proving himself to be quite an adequate wrapper even if he did lack Indie's flair for the dramatic.

By the time we opened, a small group was waiting outside, and Rocky had put out a double batch of peppermint-chocolate rolls for sale. She was going to sell out in minutes, I was sure.

A few minutes later, Stephen and Walter came in and set up their membership table again, and despite my protests, they insisted on hanging out all day. "It's so festive here, Harvey. Don't make us go sit in our plain old house," Stephen said.

Their "plain old house" featured no less than three

Christmas trees and a level of Christmas décor that was only rivaled by professional designers. But I didn't argue too hard. I liked having them around because it made me feel more festive, too.

However, when Indie came in just before ten, I tried to convince her to go home or at least spend the day with Car and Niall.

"Nope," she said. "My mom is where she needs to be to get the help she needs." She hugged me. "Thank you for that. I've been trying for years to get her to find a therapist, but she wouldn't admit she had a problem. Said she wasn't like her brother." Indie shook her head. "She wasn't like her brother, but her problems were just as deep, all rooted in the fact that she might get abandoned, left behind."

I shook my head. "Gracious. That is so hard." I paused, choosing my words carefully. "Is that why she was so concerned about you? She was worried you might get wrapped up in something and forget about her?" I'd had a sense of this idea the night before when I'd been talking to Jared while Malaysia watched. Just the idea that her daughter might need her had obviously given her such joy.

Indie nodded. "I guess. It's hard to know since it seems like she probably killed Aunt Mildred. Maybe she just didn't want me to figure that out."

"Yeah," I said. "I'm so sorry. That's a lot for you to handle."

She shrugged. "I actually think it's easier to handle things when I know what's going on, like with Komiko. Now that we've cleared the air, we're starting to talk about launching a new business. Environmental Design from architecture to interior."

"That sounds exciting, and I do know what you mean. I think that's part of why I can't stay out of the police's business —it's just easier for me if I understand things than it is to be in the dark." I hadn't thought of that before, but now that I said it, I knew it was true.

"Exactly," Indie said. "Now that I know about Uncle Car's illness and that Mildred was researching to see if she could help, I can continue her work. Besides, since my uncle and mom have serious mental health struggles, it's probably wise that I know about their illnesses if I begin to develop symptoms."

I pulled her into another hug. "Let's hope that doesn't happen." Mental illness often ran in families, but I thought it likely that Indie might be able to manage the symptoms at least, if not stave off the illness altogether, given what she now knew.

"But enough about me," she said. "Uncle Car is on his way over with Komiko. They're staffing the Mental Health Association table, and they want me to drum up some interest for them." She held up some shimmery blue package labels with the Association's logos on them. "Mind if I use these?"

"Not at all," I said. "What a great idea." And her idea gave me one of my own.

WHEN MARCUS CAME in at eleven, I excused myself to go to the back room and spent the next hour making a special addition to the steampunk window display. When I climbed in and tucked the shiny blue present tag on Cate's huge clock, Marcus sidled up to see what I was doing.

"Oh, just giving back a little more of the holiday spirit," I said. "Let's go take a look."

I waved to Rocky so she could join us, and the three of us walked outside and looked at the front window. There, in bright white letters, the tag read, "Happy Holidays, St. Marin's. Stop in for your free hot chocolate."

"I'm buying for everyone," I told the café owner.

"Oh no. You are not besting me for holiday spirit. We'll split the cost," she said.

"Actually, we'd like to contribute, too," someone said from behind us.

When I turned around, I saw Car and Niall standing there with my mom and dad. "Can we?" Car said.

I looked at Rocky, and both of us nodded. "Of course," I said. "You okay?" I asked in a more somber tone.

Car nodded, although his face looked quite sad. "I just came from the police station, and Malaysia has confessed. She lost her temper with our sister that night. She's sorry, I think, but she's also in a pretty dark place."

Niall put his arm around his fiancé. "At Car's recommendation, Tuck is asking a psychologist to come in and evaluate her. The district attorney agreed that was a good idea."

I put my hand on Car's arm. "Then she'll get the help she needs." I looked back at the window. "I just wish it hadn't taken Mildred's death."

"Me, too," Car said. "But sometimes, it takes a whole lot of shadow to bring things into the light."

The six of us stood on the sidewalk for a long moment, just taking in the bustle of Main Street. And then Niall said, "And speaking of light, Harvey, we were wondering if we could borrow your store again today."

I looked from him to Car even as I nodded.

Out of the corner of my eye, Marcus was grinning. "Are you going to do what I think you're going to do?"

"If you think we'd like to get married, then we're on the same wavelength," Car said.

"What?" I said as I looked between the grooms. "Today? In my store?"

"We can't wait, and we can't think of a better place," Niall said. "Plus, the best event planner on the Eastern Shore is coordinating for us, so I think we're in good hands."

I turned to my mom, whose face was practically beaming

with delight. "Car and Niall insist you keep the store open, though, Harvey. It's part of the charm."

Marcus and I exchanged a glance that clearly communicated, "We aren't sure this is going to work," but neither of us said a word.

"Okay, what do we need to do?" I asked, feeling a little panicky about how busy the store was and all that was going on.

"You run your store, dear," Mom said. "I've got this."

"Alrighty, then," I said as we headed back inside. "Make yourselves at home."

AT FOUR P.M. THAT AFTERNOON, Carson Radison and Niall Baker got married in a spectacular ceremony, officiated by Bear and attended by every one of our friends. Thanks to Elle's expertise, the décor was festive and bright, and the food was perfect—all Mexican pastries and desserts. Both men wore lovely suits that Max had custom tailored by his tailor up in Easton, and Pickle found a bluegrass band to provide the ceremony and the reception music. I decided that Pacabel's Canon really was best played on a banjo.

Indie was the maid of honor, and Komiko was a bridesmaid. Niall's daughter even made it up from North Carolina for the ceremony, and I had the honor of offering the first toast at the reception.

We cleared the reading space floor of chairs after the toasts and the cutting of the dulce de leche cake. Everyone danced into the late evening, including the customers who happened to wander in and took to heart the huge invitation to join us that Marcus had printed and put on a stand by the front door at the groom's request.

When "At Last" played, Jared asked me to dance, and the two of us swayed on the floor beside the two grooms.

As the song ended, he leaned over and placed his lips against my ear. "What do you think about holding our reception here?" he asked.

I thought it was the best idea in the world. "A Christmas Day wedding sound okay to you?"

"Perfect," he said as he kissed my cheek. "Absolutely perfect."

HARVEY AND MARCUS'S BOOK RECOMMENDATIONS

Here is where you will find all the books Harvey and Marcus recommend in *Picture Book Peril*. Happy Reading!

- *The Polar Express* by Chris Van Allsburg
- *Hauntings and Humbug* by Melanie Karsak
- *A Christmas Carol* by Charles Dickens
- *We Should All Be Millionaires* by Rachel Rodgers
- *Finlay Donovan Is Killing It* by Elle Cosimano
- *Necromancer* by William Gibson
- *Northern Lights* by Philip Pullman
- The Books of Babel by Josiah Bancroft
- *A Star Called Bitterness* by Trevor McCall
- *An Unquiet Mind* by Kay Redfield Jamison
- *Chapter and Curse* by Elizabeth Penney
- *A Unicorn Named Sparkle's First Christmas* by Amy Young
- *Most Marshmallows* by Rowboat Watkins
- *Atomic Habits* by James Clear
- *The Da Vinci Code* by Dan Brown
- *The Collector* by John Fowles

- *The Invisible Library* by Genevieve Cogman
- *Captain Underpants* by Dav Pilkey
- *Confessions of a Funeral Director* by Caleb Wilde
- *We Are All the Same in the Dark* by Julia Heaberlin
- *House of Hollow* by Krystal Sutherland
- *Court of Thorns and Roses* by Sarah J. Maas
- Keeper of the Lost Cities series by Shannon Messenger
- *Piranesi* by Susanna Clarke
- *Little Devil in America* by Hanif Abdurraqib
- *The Chinese in America* by Iris Chang
- *You Are a Badass at Making Money* by Jenn Sincero
- First 100 Box Set by Roger Priddy
- *The Storied Life of A.J. Fikry* by Gabrielle Zevin
- *Outlander* by Diana Gabaldon

A FREE COZY SET IN SAN FRANCISCO

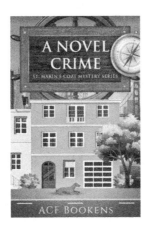

Join my Cozy Up email group for weekly book recommendations & a FREE copy of *A Novel Crime*, the prequel to my St. Marin's Cozy Mystery Series.
Sign up here - https://bookens.andilit.com/CozyUp

ALSO BY ACF BOOKENS

St. Marin's Cozy Mystery Series

Publishable By Death

Entitled To Kill

Bound To Execute

Plotted For Murder

Tome To Tomb

Scripted To Slay

Proof Of Death

Epilogue of An Epitaph

Hardcover Homicide

Picture Book Peril

Dog-Eared Danger - Coming June 2023

Stitches In Crime Series

Crossed By Death

Bobbins and Bodies

Hanged By A Thread

Counted Corpse

Stitch X For Murder

Sewn At The Crime

Blood And Backstitches

Fatal Floss

Strangled Skein

Aida Time

Poe Baxter Books Series

Fatalities And Folios

Massacre And Margins

Butchery And Bindings

Monograph and Murder - Coming in February 2023

Spines and Slaughter - Coming in March 2023

ABOUT THE AUTHOR

ACF Bookens lives in Virginia's Southwestern Mountains with her young son, an old hound, and a bully mix who has already eaten two couches. When she's not writing, she cross-stitches, watches YA fantasy shows, and grows massive quantities of cucumbers. Find her at acfbookens.com.